Dinosaur Tracks
and Murder

Dinosaur Tracks and Murder

John Dellinger

Northwest Publishing, Inc.
Salt Lake City, Utah

Dinosaur Tracks and Murder

For information address: Northwest Publishing, Inc.
6906 South 300 West, Salt Lake City, Utah 84047

JC 08 10 94

PRINTING HISTORY
First Printing 1995

ISBN: 1-56901-307-1

NPI books are published by Northwest Publishing, Incorporated,
6906 South 300 West, Salt Lake City, Utah 84047.
The name "NPI" and the "NPI" logo are trademarks belonging to
Northwest Publishing, Incorporated.

PRINTED IN THE UNITED STATES OF AMERICA.
10 9 8 7 6 5 4 3 2 1

One

Nineteen forty-nine was a good year. There aren't many good years. Most are filled with floods and famine, wars and rumors of wars, too many heartburns and not enough Pepto Bismol. Then again, I guess it all comes down to where you were and what you were doing during a particular year—if you know what I mean.

In 1949 I had a little office stashed in between two used car lots on West Colfax, on the outskirts of Denver. There weren't too many car lots and there wasn't much of an outskirt. Frank Brodrick's Motel, the Pig and Poke—where Frank, a one-time fighter and sparring partner of heavyweight champs, served up coffee, grub, and the room where I lived—was probably the most prominent feature of the street. A new Mailer's Supermarket, where you pushed food around in little black-wheeled green carts with wire baskets you took off the carts and placed on the checkout counter, was also a big attraction. There were other businesses running up and down the street; they dwindled into nothingness towards the mountains, leaving most of the fifteen-mile gap from my motel room to the city of Golden and the mountains in the west unfilled.

Well, you get the picture—it wasn't much, but so what? It was home and it was a good time to be alive. In my business I sometimes come into contact with those who aren't alive.

"Give me the keys to the '49 Hudson, Joe."

"Ah, Marty, not again." Joe's displeasure was apparent as he rolled from side to side the stub of black cigar that burned dangerously near his lips. I waited patiently with my left hand in the pocket of my light blue sports coat that went well with my dark blue trousers. A white shirt, without tie, and unbuttoned top button, completed the day's attire.

"Yes, again," I said with no show of emotion. Joe Galliger owed me. I had cleaned up a sticky situation for him that had involved the northside mob. Without me, he wouldn't have had any cars; maybe he wouldn't have even had his life. I didn't let him forget it and took it out in borrowing whatever I pleased from his car lot. The red Hudson convertible was the newest thing he had on the lot, only three months old. I had driven it four, maybe five times. I wasn't tired of it yet.

"They found one of my former clients dead, up by the Hogback. What she was doing up there, I don't know. Maybe if I get there before they cart the body away, I can figure out what happened. I'll take the keys now."

Galliger's graying red eyebrow on the right side of his face raised in annoyance more than anger as he reached toward the rack of keys behind him. He was mumbling his usual, "Be careful, Marty," plea as I pulled onto West Colfax with the top down. The plea was for the car, not for me.

I liked the feel of the Hudson. It was a good solid car with a body that hugged the ground with a long straight line that extended back to a tail that ran low and easy over the road.

Running boards were gone and the gearshift had been moved from the floor up to the steering column. Cars had really advanced in the last couple of years. I didn't see how they could get much better. The Hudson gave me luxuriant pleasure as I felt the wind blowing through my almost-marine-short black hair.

I hadn't let the hair completely grow out since the end of the war. In some ways, I was still back on Iwo Jima, but so what? Wasn't practically every guy these days still hung up somewhere in the war, even though it had been over for four years.

Times were good, and the war was far away, but it never got much further away than the five-inch scar that cut into my right shoulder blade. I couldn't see it on my back, but I could feel it, always reminding me of how lucky I was to be alive.

After the war I had grown an Errol Flynn mustache; guys with short black hair could have thin black mustaches. The blue eyes didn't necessarily go with the black hair and not-so-fair complexion, but maybe that was the German showing through the Indian, English, and Irish. I always looked tan in summer or winter, more tan in summer than winter. My eyes were always the same color of deep-lake dark blue.

I used my right hand to tap out a Lucky from the pack and lit it with the car lighter that I pulled from the dash. I fiddled with the dial on the radio and found a little dance music. I was relaxing and blowing smoke rings, but the music made me think of Irene.

The wind coming into the open convertible blew the smoke rings apart and carried them away almost as soon as they had formed. That was the way Irene's life had been. Like a vapor, she had vanished all too soon.

Just a year younger than me, Irene had become a twenty-nine-year-old dead divorcee. She had been a knockout red-head with green eyes and peach-colored skin that didn't have the freckles most redheads have. She was as beautiful as a woman could be.

I didn't know how her husband could have fooled around

on her, but I had caught him at it. I had broken his nose when he threatened me in an attempt to keep me quiet, but that hardly seemed motive enough to kill her.

When I arrived, police cars were lined up on the side of the road in the early-morning Colorado sun. Maybe I shouldn't have taken the Hudson convertible. I sneezed twice before I got out of the car. It was going to be a bad day for hay fever. June was one of my worst months.

They had already loaded her body into the black Cadillac hearse by the time I had walked up the road past the police cars and to the dinosaur tracks.

"What can you tell me, Harry?"

"Strange, Marty, real strange. A lot of blood on the sandstone right here and on her, but she wasn't bleeding. She was strangled. The body was propped up against the stone in a sitting position. I speculate the blood came from whoever propped her up."

"Simple then," I said. "Find the owner of the blood and you've got the murderer."

"Maybe so, but why here, under the dinosaur tracks?"

He pointed up to the indentations in the parchment-colored stone. The indentations were about fifteen feet up in the sheet of flat stone that lay against the mountainside. Erosion had cut away the outer layers of the stone, revealing the tracks that a local professor had identified as dinosaur tracks, left millions of years before when the stone had not yet hardened. Some geologists referred to them as "footprints" rather than "tracks," but I didn't see that it made much difference. Whatever you called them, they were evidence of the huge creatures that had once inhabited the area.

Somebody had given the name "Hogback" to the small mountain that was a fold out from the other foothills. I suppose they thought the top of the mountain that stood alone resembled the back of a hog. Maybe it was the paved road that had been carved in a straight line ascending the mountain that was really like going up the back of a sitting hog. The road started at a bottom corner of the mountain and climbed steadily along the outside of the mountain. When it reached the top corner, you had a forty-five-degree triangle from the bottom of the mountain to the top, with the base of the mountain being the bottom of the triangle. The vegetation of the mountain was unimpressive. Small pine trees and bushes were spaced far apart, with wild grass and rock filling in the spaces.

"Maybe they were sightseeing," I suggested.

"In the middle of the night?" Harry used the thumb and forefinger on his left hand to stroke his black mustache that was similar to mine. He was a Greek type, with round, olive-black eyes and delicate features. I weighed over 180 pounds and was a shade over six feet. "Harry couldn't have weighed more than 150 pounds and couldn't have been more than 5'8". He always wore a dark gray suit from his collection of three of the same. His tie was usually gray. Even though he had been in the army instead of the marines, he was an O.K. guy—good cop too.

"Shouldn't be too hard to pin a motive on that ex-husband of hers from what you told me about their divorce, but why here, Marty?" He continued to stroke his mustache while looking at me for an answer.

"I don't know. Maybe they were up here parked in the car and he was trying to get her out of her bra. Sometimes divorced couples get the hots for each other and it draws them back together. They could have been looking out at the lights of the city from Lovers' Point, up the road a couple of hundred yards from here. Romance led to a fight and he killed her."

"And brought the body here?" Harry looked at me totally unconvinced.

"Well, I'll let you know if I turn up anything in my travels through the city. Mind if I hang around here with you for awhile?"

"Why should I mind?"

"You shouldn't. I just thought I'd ask for once."

Harry and I didn't turn up much after the hearse and the other cops left. We walked the road up to the overlook, looking for signs of struggle or torn clothes. Nothing, not even at Lovers' Point that offered a perfect view of Denver in the distance and dropped into a nearly straight fall of a couple hundred feet.

Harry was standing with his hands in the trouser pockets of his dark gray suit and looking at the fuzzy outline of Denver when he spoke. "If he would have killed her here, he would have just thrown her over. Maybe the body wouldn't have been discovered for days. No corpse, no murder charge."

I agreed, but I couldn't see the connection between a beautiful dead redhead and dinosaur tracks that were millions of years old. Did the dinosaur tracks have something to do with the murder or was it just coincidental that the body was found so close to the indentations in the rock?

On the way back to town I was listening to the radio and they played the song "Good Night, Irene." The song had been played so much that practically everyone in the country knew the words by heart. "Good night, Irene, good night, Irene; I'll see you in my dreams."

As I hummed along with the song I knew I would see her in my dreams—very beautiful and very dead. Was it her ex-husband? If the cops couldn't pin it on him, then I would. Maybe he didn't do it. Whoever it was, I was going to make sure somebody paid for what they had done to Irene. Good night, Irene—dead, but not forgotten.

Two

Harry let me have a crack at the ex-husband after the cops had gone over him. Harry was with me when I verbally chewed on a member of one of Denver's most prominent families. He had been in the war too, an officer in the paratroopers. He had good manners, good education, and good looks, in spite of the bend I had put in his nose when I had broken it. His jaw, untouched by my fists, was strong and lean, looking like one side of a perfect square. His blond, wavy hair didn't even sweat under the hot white light that showered down from the gray cone-shaped light fixture. The chocolate-brown pin-striped suit and chocolate-brown tie he had been arrested in should have made him sweat.

"What do you mean you didn't see her until after she was dead?"

His pale blue eyes looked at Harry. "Do I have to endure more of this clown?" He shuffled the wooden chair on the cement floor as if he wanted to get up.

"Humor him," Harry said with the outside corners of his eyes creased in amusement. "Sometimes he gets real bright. If you give him anything to go on, he might prove your innocence."

Barry Hampton's attitude toward me abruptly changed. "You working for anybody now?"

"I'm always working for somebody, but on this particular case, no."

"Five thousand if you prove my story and get me off."

I almost whistled with joy at the offer of five grand, but I managed an outward display of calm.

"If it's true, I'll prove it. If it's not, you can take a seat in the electric chair. Let's hear the whole story once more."

I knew the story by heart, but I would continue watching his face for eye movements and expressions that might display guilt or untruth. So far, his performance had been flawless, but five big ones seemed like a lot for an innocent man to offer someone to prove his innocence.

"O.K., one more time. Irene called me."

"You mean you called her," I interjected.

"No, she called me."

My thrust had been awkward, and I wouldn't try any more. This guy was smooth and smart. I wouldn't trip him up with any simple ploy.

The story remained the same. She had called him and asked to meet him at Lovers' Point about midnight. Lovers' Point was a place that held fond memories for them because it was where they had gone on their first date. She had said it was urgent that he be there. He arrived and she wasn't there.

After waiting an hour for her, he decided to leave. On the way back down the Hogback he had seen someone sitting by the side of the road. He had stopped the car and found Irene dead. He had attempted to lift her body and place it in his car.

The roadside was slick from a recent rain. He had slipped

on the wet stones and wet grass, falling and bumping the nose that I had put a break in over a year ago. The nose had bled profusely.

His blood on Irene had caused him to panic. He thought he would be accused of her death. He had propped her up into a sitting position again and left.

"Any idea who might want to strangle her?"

The pain in his face when I talked about her strangulation suggested to me that he still cared a great deal about her even though they were divorced. Maybe he had cared enough to kill her.

"She seemed to be well-liked by everyone. I have no idea why anyone would kill her. She was a very lovely person."

"Why did you fool around on her?"

He glared at me. "Let's not drag that up. I was tempted by another woman. I gave into temptation. It's as simple as that. You like beautiful women, don't you?"

"Yes, I like beautiful women, but if I would have had a beautiful doll like Irene, you wouldn't have caught me fooling around with anyone else."

The comment seemed to hurt him and I backed off.

"O.K., Hampton, I'm working to prove your innocence for five thousand bucks. If the cops or I prove your guilt, I'll chalk it up to experience. That will come free of charge. I've got a dog-bite case that should keep me in hamburgers for awhile."

Barry Hampton looked at me with piercing pale blue eyes. "Well, Mayfield, maybe you are an O.K. guy and will believe me. I honestly didn't do it. I hope you get the bastard who did it. I loved Irene and I want the real murderer caught. I'd like to get my hands on whoever did it."

I looked at him and I believed him enough to give him the benefit of the doubt. Besides, five grand buys a lot of credibility.

"Here's one of my business cards," I said, handing him the little white card that had MARTIN MAYFIELD—PRIVATE INVESTIGATIONS on it. It also contained the telephone number of Joe Galliger's car lot. I couldn't afford a secretary.

"As a client, you've got a right to know where to reach me. It also pays to advertise."

Harry stifled a laugh. He knew how poor my business practices were and how Joe Galliger sometimes didn't see me for hours or days to give me messages.

"Harry, I suppose you think I should be listed in the yellow pages."

"No, Marty, I'm sure your office staff does a more-than-adequate job of keeping your clients and potential clients informed." He laughed.

I was tempted to say something in reply, but I didn't want to act unprofessional in front of a client.

Barry Hampton looked relieved to have someone working on the case, even though I knew he would hire the best lawyers in the city to defend himself. Lawyers know how to read law books, but they usually don't know much about detective work. Barry was lucky to have me. I just might get lucky myself and make five thousand dollars, if he was telling the truth. Then again, if he had knocked her off, he deserved to be stir-fried in grease and the five thousand could rot in hell with him.

Three

I didn't turn up anything in the next two days that either proved or disproved Barry Hampton's guilt or innocence. When I dropped by the police station in answer to the message Harry Makris had sent for me to come in, I didn't know any more about the case than I had when I had left the station two days before.

"We're going to let Hampton go, Marty. I wanted to fill you in on why and give you a chance to talk to him before he's back on the streets. You still might collect that five thousand bucks from him if he thinks you had something to do with getting him out and if he thinks we still suspect him. He's still a remote suspect, but I think he's clean. I couldn't hold him much longer anyway. His lawyers are screaming for us to either let him go or charge him. They'll slap us with a writ of habeas corpus if I hold him much longer. But I don't see much point in holding him anyway. As I said, I don't think he's our murderer."

"Why do you think he's clean?" I asked as I sat down on the corner of Harry's desk.

"Do you mind, Marty? I'm supposed to look like you're just another citizen who might be of help to us, not my good buddy. The captain doesn't like me feeding you inside police information anyway."

"Sorry, Harry," I said as I moved into the wooden chair beside the desk and tried to look more like John Q. Citizen.

"Irene Hampton's father was murdered last night at about midnight while Barry Hampton was in jail. We fished the elderly George Berkowitz out of Sloan's Lake at daybreak. One of the residents near the lake saw him take the fall. Just enough moonlight to see somebody pump three shots into the professor and drop him over the side of the boat dock, but not enough to get a description of the assailant."

"What if the murders aren't connected?" I asked while lighting a Lucky with a match from the matchbook that read "Red Horse Bar and Grill." I liked the picture of the red stallion in full flight on the white cover.

Harry pushed his chair back to avoid my smoke rings. He was a non-smoker who didn't like to be near the stuff.

"'It would be an awful big coincidence if they weren't. What do you think are the odds of both a daughter and a father being murdered by two different assailants? They might be murdered at separate times, but there is probably a very strong connection between the two murders. Otherwise, it's just too coincidental."

"You said he was a professor. A professor of what?"

"Geology. School of Mines in Golden. George Berkowitz was 'the authority' on geology in the Rocky Mountain region. He had mapped, or whatever they call it, most of the geology in Colorado and other Rocky Mountain states. The people at the School of Mines tell me he will be sorely missed."

"What was he doing at Sloan's Lake in the middle of the night?"

Harry shook his head. "I haven't a clue, and that's literal. No suspects, no leads at present. All I can tell you is that the murder weapon was a .45, we think. The lab is working on it."

Harry signaled a uniformed police officer. "Have them release Barry Hampton. Bring him up here and then fill out the paperwork. I want to talk to him before he goes."

Barry Hampton appeared in less than five minutes. Harry and I took him into "The Pit," the interrogation room, for a chat before he was released. It was the same room where we had questioned him the last time.

"Well, Hampton, I'm releasing you into Mr. Mayfield's custody.'"

Hampton blinked in surprise.

"Mr. Mayfield has led me to doubt your guilt, somewhat. You're not off the hook yet. You could still be guilty as sin, but I think there is a reasonable enough doubt that we can let you go without charging you and having you put up bail. Just keep in touch with Mr. Mayfield and he'll let me know what else he turns up."

Hampton looked at me with what I took to be a look of surprised respect. "What did you turn up, Mayfield?"

"A few confidential things, known to me and the police department. You understand I can't let you in on everything; it might spoil the relationship of trust I have with the police department that comes in handy at a time like this. I will tell you that I've convinced Mr. Makris here that two murders in the same family don't add up to a conviction for a suspect who was in jail when one of the murders was committed."

"Two murders?"

"You want me to tell him about the second one, Harry?"

"I'll tell him. I was going to question him about it before he left. Your former father-in-law, we fished him out of Sloan's Lake this morning, pumped full of lead."

Barry Hampton looked stressed, but not totally broken up as a close family member might be.

"Nice old guy; who would want to kill him? Even though Irene and I split up, I had nothing but the highest regard for him."

"Indeed, Mr. Hampton," Harry said, "who would want to kill him?"

"I have no idea, just as I have no idea who would want to kill Irene. A perfectly charming old gentleman who was quite an authority on the local geology."

"Yes, we know," Harry interjected, wanting to get to the meat of anything Barry Hampton might say. "Any enemies, any quarrels, any connection with his daughter other than usual father-daughter; anything special about his geology or business dealings? Give me anything you've got, Hampton. What made him special enough that somebody might want to bump him off?"

"I don't know. As I said, he was a leading authority on the state's geology. That's the only thing I know that made him special."

"Geology could be a motive for murder, or it could lead to a motive," Harry said. Harry's thumb played with his thin black mustache as he thought and spoke. That was about the only annoying habit he had. "Geology means important minerals. Gold and silver made this state. People have always been willing to kill for precious metals. Did Irene have any connection to mineral wealth or her father's expertise on minerals?"

"Not that I know of. She was close to her father, but I don't think she knew much about or had much of an interest in geology. She admired the rock collection I showed her from my boyhood days, but that was about it as far as I could tell."

"Work on it, Marty," Harry said, raising his voice to me. "Keep a close eye on your client Mr. Hampton here, and keep me informed of this or any other leads you follow up on. Remember, I'm only letting him out because of you. You owe me and he owes you. Good police work, Marty."

"Thanks, Harry." I smiled. "You probably would have come up with the logic on the two murders anyway. Maybe it was just because I wanted to get my client out of jail that I got to it so fast. When I'm working for five thousand bucks, I can think pretty fast."

Harry continued the charade. "Remember, he's not off the hook, just released in your custody. He could have paid someone to knock off the professor while he was in here. I don't think he did or else I wouldn't let him go. Now, both of you, get out of here before I change my mind. Stop by the desk sergeant to sign the necessary release forms on the way out."

"Sure thing, Harry."

I nudged Barry Hampton through the door of "The Pit." Hampton couldn't see the wink I gave Harry as I said, "I owe you one at the Red Horse."

Hampton wasn't ready to part with the five thousand yet, but he was grateful enough to ask me to stop off at his downtown bank so that he could write me out a check for a grand for the "good work I had done so far." When Barry Hampton handed me the check, I was sitting behind the wheel of the black '41 Mercury coupe with wide white sidewalls I had borrowed to drive to the police station that morning. The sun was shining on me in more ways than one.

"Thanks, Mayfield. So far, you're better than I thought you would be. Clear me out of this mess and I'll give you the other four thousand. As you make progress, I'll give you more money. Ever do any bodyguard work?"

"How do you think I managed to break your nose? I've been known to take care of myself and my clients. You're safe when you're with me."

Hampton looked annoyed. "No, not me. Probably just a lucky punch anyway." He felt his nose with the fingers of his right hand.

I didn't spoil his illusion of grandeur. After all, the man had just handed me a check for a thousand dollars.

"Probably just a lucky punch," I agreed. "Who's the innocent?"

"The innocent?"

"The person you want me to protect," I said patiently.

"You did say something about bodyguarding, didn't you? You've got to remember, this may tie me down a bit on your case. If I'm holding somebody's hand, I won't be as free to roam on your case."

"You just hold her hand when she is out and about. I'll see to it that she is safely locked in when she is at home. Her name is Audrey and Irene was her sister."

"Why do you think she needs protecting?"

"You figure it out. First Irene, and then her father. Audrey is the only one left in the family. The mother died about ten years ago. Don't you think Audrey might be in danger?"

"You've got a point. Is it worth another fifty bucks a day to you? Being a bodyguard can be dangerous at times, especially in light of what has happened to her recent blood relatives. I'll take her with me during the day and you tuck her in at night. I hope she's not ugly. I have a reputation to maintain."

Hampton smiled. "Your reputation is safe. Neither she nor Irene ever had an ugly bone in their bodies. Fifty dollars per day, in addition to the five thousand you are working on. But if you get the killer, dead or alive, the fifty dollars per day is included in the five thousand."

"Why is it you want to protect her?" I asked while searching his face for a reaction.

"I loved Irene. She is Irene's sister. Good enough?"

"Good enough," I said as I pulled the shiny black Mercury out into downtown traffic and bright sunshine.

Four

Audrey Berkowitz was as beautiful as her sister had been. At twenty-seven she had never married, a mystery to me how such a beautiful woman could go unattached that long.

It was nearing three o'clock in the afternoon when I parked in front of her house. I had done some background checking and had a leisurely lunch and a stiff drink before taking up my bodyguarding duties. I had also taken time to cash the thousand-dollar check Hampton had given me. It felt good to pay the back rent on my room and office, plus put over six hundred dollars in my iron office safe.

She lived two blocks from the Colorado School of Mines in what had been the family home. It was a red-brick two-story, probably built during the 1870s or 1880s when Golden was still vying with its neighbor Denver, about fifteen miles to the east, for state prominence. Denver had won, becoming the political and commercial capital of the state, but Golden, nestled at the foot of the mountains, was far more picturesque and small-town pleasant.

Audrey shared some of her father's bent for science and had become a teacher of science at the local high school. Since it was summer vacation, her time was her own. She didn't like the idea of being baby-sat, and although the recent deaths of her sister and father had upset her emotionally, she was capable of spitting a little venom my way.

"I don't need you to protect me," she said sharply.

"Come now, Miss Berkowitz," I said as reassuringly as I could, "your sister's former husband thinks you might be in danger. I must say I agree."

"Barry called and said he was sending you out. As I told him, I don't need protecting. Go away!"

I expected her to slam the door in my face at any moment. Instead, she continued to peek out from the side of the solid, heavy wood door that was fastened with a heavy iron night chain.

"I understand how you wouldn't want to see anyone at this time," I continued in my calm, reassuring tone. "Won't you at least come out or let me in so we can talk about whether or not you might be in danger. Here's my card. You can see what I do for a living. Call the police department in Denver and ask for Detective Harry Makris. He'll vouch for me."

She took the card I handed her through the partially opened door. I could hear the night chain rattle as she undid it and it came down against the door. The door swung open.

I walked in. I don't quite know how it happened, but she ended up in my arms. The tears were flowing freely. I had shaved and put on my black suit with white pin-stripes, white shirt, and ruby-red tie before coming out, wanting to make a good impression, but I didn't expect this much response. When I wore the suit to weddings or funerals, which is where I usually wore it, women hardly leaped into my arms.

"Yes, I am afraid. It's awful, so awful. How could any-one..." She couldn't bring herself to say it—I knew she was referring to the murders of her sister and father.

"You poor kid," I said and I meant it. "You must be going through so much."

I let her cry for a long while and then gently moved her toward a seat on the couch. Normally, a beautiful woman in my arms would have caused me to get romantically interested in her, but I could only feel sorrow for Audrey Berkowitz.

I sat diagonally across from her in the easy chair. I wanted to observe her and gauge her appearance and emotions. I had learned to be observant and it helped me more than any police blotter I ever read.

When I looked at her I liked what I saw. She was long and leggy, with light-brown, almost blonde hair, worn fashion-ably straight to the shoulders. Her hair had a radiant look. Her eyes were the same color of green as her sister's had been. She would look good in anything—or nothing. Currently, she was wearing a navy-blue, pleated skirt, white blouse and no socks or shoes. As she spoke, she curled her bare feet up on the couch beside her, hiding all but a delicately curved instep of one of them under her navy-blue skirt which she had draped on the couch beside her. Her pair of black flat shoes lay on the floor in front of the couch, ready to be slipped on by her if she wanted to go someplace.

"I'm sorry, Mr. Mayfield, for that outburst. You must think me awful." She was daubing at her beautiful green eyes with a large blue handkerchief she had taken from the end table. Her eyes and the handkerchief looked as if she had been crying long before I got there.

"This has upset me so. And I am grateful. I suppose I do need someone to guard me. It is so terrible. Why should anyone want to do what they did to my sister and father?"

"That, Miss Berkowitz, is something I would like to know." I smiled reassuringly at her. "So far, the only thing I've been able to figure out as a possible motive is geology, but maybe it is something entirely different. Anybody have a grudge against your family? Any past or present acquaintances who were angry at you or your family?"

"No, I can't think of anyone who disliked any of us. My father and I have both given failing grades to some of our students who weren't happy about them, but it seems ridiculous that anyone would be unhappy enough over a grade to..."

"Distraught relatives? Family inheritance at stake? Anything like that?"

"No. We are not a rich family, and we have few close relatives. My father was an only child. Most of my mother's relatives are back east and we haven't had much contact with them since she died quite some time ago."

"Well, let's use geology as a possible motive. Was your father working on anything or connected with anything that might be worth something to somebody? I mean, like worth a lot of money. Something worth enough to..." I started to say, "kill for," but I changed the wording to "want to get their hands on it?"

"Dad was recently doing a lot of work on uranium."

"You mean the stuff they use in atomic bombs and that sort of thing?"

"Yes. Over on the Western Slope, around Rangely, they have been developing some uranium mines. With the Russians and the Cold War, uranium has become a very important concern of national security. But I really don't think Dad had anything to do with the actual mining. He has been involved in locating geological formations that are most likely to contain uranium."

"How about your sister, did she have anything to do with that sort of thing?"

"Oh, my goodness, no. Irene never was much on science. She worked for a downtown Denver bank after college. She gave it up when she married Barry. She returned to the bank when she and Barry split up. She was with the real estate loan department, mostly houses. Banks have been doing a lot of G.I. loans with the G.I. Bill. Were you in the war, Mr. Mayfield?"

"Wasn't everybody?" I said, wanting not to discuss the war or my part in it. "So, there could be a tie-in between your father's death and uranium? Maybe the Russians wanted it or wanted to shut him up about whatever he knew about uranium."

"Do you really think there could be a tie-in with the Russians and what my father knew about uranium? Does everything relate to the Cold War these days?"

"Well, you figure it out. The Russians tried to block us out of Berlin. We countered with the Berlin Airlift. Europe is a powderkeg, set to go up at any minute. The U.S. and Russia are competing for supremacy in atomic weapons. Uranium is what they use to build atomic bombs. Your father was an expert on uranium. It seems as plausible as anything we've got to go on."

"But what about my sister Irene? She didn't know anything about uranium."

"Maybe she knew enough about something connected with it. Or maybe your father confided in her as to what he had found or whatever he was working on. Somebody thought she knew enough to kill her."

As soon as the words were out of my mouth I regretted using them. Audrey, although trying to hold back tears, went on a crying jag again. I sat beside her on the couch and put my arms around her. I held her for a long time and let her cry herself out.

Regaining some composure, she asked, "Shouldn't we tell the F.B.I. or somebody about what we suspect? If the Cold War is what caused this, wouldn't they be interested?"

"They would, but so far we haven't got much to go on, just a theory. Let's nose around a bit and see what we come up with. It might be something entirely different from what we suspect. In the meantime, we've got to make sure nothing happens to you."

She looked approvingly at me. "Thanks, Mr. Mayfield."

"Marty will do," I said. Although we were quite close, I resisted the urge to kiss those beautiful lips that were only inches away from my own. Instead, I pulled away, stood, and reached inside my shirt pocket for my pack of Luckies.

"Mind if I smoke?"

"Why should I? I'll get you an ash tray."

I offered her a cigarette before lighting my own. She refused. "No, I haven't taken up the habit. I have a few suspicions that it might be worse for you than people think. Then, maybe it's just because I'm an old-maid science teacher. I don't see how breathing that smoke into your lungs could not be bad for you."

"Nah, it won't hurt you," I said, taking a deep drag on the Lucky. "If it's so bad for you, why are all of those doctors in those cigarette ads telling you what they smoke?"

"Well, you have a point. Smoke if you like, but remember it may be bad for you."

"We just met, and already you're worried about my health," I said with a smile and a wink of my left eye. "You might be my kind of woman, but if anything happens to my lungs, it will probably be from somebody pumping lead into them."

"You mean being shot?"

"Yes, shot, a bullet, whatever you want to call it. But I learned in the war, that it doesn't matter. When it's your time to go, you go. If it's not your time to go, you won't."

"Kind of fatalistic, isn't it?" she said with a smile of her own. "If that's the case, why are you guarding me? Couldn't I do just as well on my own?"

I started to ponder that, but before I could do much with it, the door burst open. Why hadn't we locked it when I had come in? It must have been her in my arms that caused me to be careless.

I hit one of the three guys as he grabbed for Audrey, knocking the pistol he was holding and him over the couch. I elbowed a second guy in the gut just as the third guy slammed the butt of his revolver down on the back of my head. It was a quick trip to dreamland where uranium glowed green in my dark mind as someone kicked me in the stomach.

Five

When I regained consciousness the couch was in flames and fire was transferring from the couch to the hanging green drape by the window. It must have been the cigarette that fell from my mouth when I slugged the first guy. Smoking could be dangerous to your health.

As I tried to clear my head I crawled toward the door. I felt lousy, but I knew I would feel a lot worse if I didn't get out of there.

Using the doorknob to pull myself up, I stood and tried the door. It was locked, apparently with a key. The bastards had meant for me to burn to death.

I looked through the smoke to make sure that wasn't the fate they had also intended for Audrey. Seeing no sign of her,

I assumed they had her with them. Otherwise, why wouldn't they have just shot us when they came in?

I ran and dived through the window, shattering the glass with the elbows and forearms I threw up in front of my face. Had I had time to think about it, I probably would have worried about cutting an artery.

I didn't cut an artery and I didn't burn up in a raging house fire. It just wasn't my time to go.

I decided it was my time to get out of there before fire trucks and the police showed up. They would detain me and ask a thousand questions that I did not want to answer. I wanted to get after Audrey and the guys who had taken her as soon as I could.

As I slipped behind the wheel of the '41 Mercury black coupe I had driven to Audrey's, I took a second to pull off the ruby-red tie. It had been ripped on my dive out the window. The black suit with the white pin-stripes had some smudges on it from the fire, but that was the advantage of wearing black, unlike the white shirt that didn't look as clean as when I had started. So much for a guy trying to look his best when meeting an attractive woman.

The Merc spun gravel as I pulled away from Audrey's street and headed for the main street in Golden. I knew I didn't have much chance of catching them, but if they were anywhere to be seen, I had the car to do it. Mercury had come on the market in 1939 with cars that I considered luxury, souped-up versions of Ford. The '41 Merc I was driving had over 63,000 miles on it, but its 95-horsepower engine was still hot enough to catch about anything on the road, except maybe some of the '49 models that had completely revolutionized car design. The white side wall tires added to its glistening black beauty that complemented the powerful rumbling purr of its engine. The one-seated coupe model was, in my opinion, one of the most attractive car designs on the road.

I was in luck. I spotted them in a green '47 Chevrolet four-door sedan. They were driving down Main real slow and easy so as not to attract attention. The driver was the only one in the front seat. The other two guys sat in the back with Audrey in the middle. She didn't appear to be struggling, probably had a gun poked in her ribs.

One of the guys spotted me as he glanced over his shoulder. I knew he had seen me because of the way the Chevrolet accelerated. I stepped on the gas pedal, and in less than two minutes we were racing up Highway 40.

I would have caught them on the uphill grade, but a gravel truck turned onto the road, nearly causing me to swerve off the road. Before I could get around the damn thing, they were cresting the hill.

They must not have been as familiar with the area as I was or they wouldn't have turned off to Red Rocks Park. Then again, maybe they thought they stood a better chance of ditching me in the park than they stood of outrunning me on the open road.

When we entered the park road, that wound through the giant pink, almost-red rocks that stuck up in the air like the spines of the ancient dinosaurs that once roamed the area, I was closing fast on them. They abandoned the car at the amphitheater and tried to lose themselves in the small number of summer tourists who had come to see the magnificent outdoor theater that had been carved during the 1930s and early 1940s as a part of the government's make-work response to the Depression. The ancient Romans would have been proud of the design—it had a seating capacity of thousands and stretched upward for several hundred feet from the outdoor stage below.

I had no trouble keeping track of the four of them as they descended a center aisle of the theater, one brown suit, two light gray suits, and Audrey in her navy-blue skirt and white blouse. I knew the area well, so I had no trouble short cutting them by going down the right side. I was waiting for them as they reached the stage area.

"All right, you can let her go and turn yourselves over to me." I held my .38 inside the right pocket of my suit coat, but they could see the outline of the barrel under the black cloth with white pin-stripes as I pointed it toward them. They chose to go for their rods instead.

Shots reverberated in the amphitheater. I dropped one of them in a gray suit with a clean shot to the chest as I dropped to one knee. A bullet skidded across my left forearm as I put the guy in the brown suit down with a bullet in the shoulder. That left a remaining gray suit to deal with.

He was shielding himself with Audrey as he went toward the exiting path on the left. He said nothing, but I knew what he meant by holding the barrel of his pistol to the temple of Audrey's head. People were screaming all over the place.

That is how we went out of the amphitheater. He backed his way out with Audrey as a shield. I followed warily at a distance, trying to stay close enough to keep contact, but staying far enough back so that he wouldn't do something stupid, like shoot Audrey.

We ended up above the amphitheater with no place to go but out on one of the red rocks. He backed toward the edge and held Audrey's and his life precariously close to falling.

"'Drop your gun or over she goes," he called in a decidedly foreign accent. I was about forty feet away.

"You're bluffing. You want her alive as much as I do. You kill her and she's no good to you. You might as well give her up because all we're going to do is wait for the police."

He shoved her aside and started firing. His aim was not as good as mine. He vanished from my view as he fell over the side. Audrey was shaking in my arms as we looked down at the lifeless body that had just missed the edge of the amphitheater and was sprawled face down on one of the smaller red rocks. A few tourists were moving toward the body and looking up.

I didn't have time to enjoy the sweetness of the moment.

"You may release her now and accompany me." The accent was as foreign as that of the guy who had just taken the big fall. It was the guy in the brown suit I had put down with a bullet to the shoulder.

He looked a lot like Peter Lorre, the movie actor, only bigger. He had a round German face with a full head of almost gray hair, combed straight back. He had round blue eyes which must have made him a perfect candidate for Hitler's master race. He was bleeding from the right shoulder where I had winged him. The pistol was in his right hand and his left hand was over the wound.

"You might bleed to death if we go anywhere."

"Not likely. I've lost a little blood, but it is not as serious as it looks. I survived worse on the Russian front in the war. Drop your pistol and move quickly before I return the favor and shoot you. We will see how well you survive a bullet."

"Too bad I wasn't a better shot," I said as Audrey and I started to move away from the edge of the rock and toward him.

"Be very careful," he continued in the same wheezing foreign accent. "You, I do not need. The lady, I prefer to keep alive. I can shoot both of you if necessary."

I said nothing as we descended the rock while I waited my chance for a way out. Coming around the other side of the rock, we did not have to descend into the amphitheater where the people were. I figured additional shots might bring people and that was probably why he hadn't shot me yet; then again, maybe he wanted to question me to see what I knew and where I fit into the picture. He motioned us into my car.

I drove the Mercury as he sat on the outside. Audrey was in the middle between us. His gun was in her ribs. I took seriously his warning of, "You drive or the lady will be shot." I knew he wanted her alive, but if it became too dangerous for him, he would try to cut his losses and run, which meant shooting both of us.

We went to a house in central Denver, only a couple of blocks from the state capitol. It was a large, expensive house, built when silver was king in Colorado in the late 1800s. Silver had crashed, but the mansions and almost-mansions the silver boom had built were still there. A couple of thugs, one as big as an ox, the other small and wiry, joined us in the driveway before we even got out of the car. This left me with no chance to make the move I had been planning.

I decided I had nothing to lose by telling them most of what I knew. It could come out of me the easy way or the hard way. I knew that easy was better than having it beaten out of me.

"I'm just a private detective hired to protect Audrey; that's all, nothing more."

"Who hired you?" one of the torpedoes asked in good American English and accent.

"Her former brother-in-law, pal, just like somebody hired you."

It was the big guy who was doing the questioning and he didn't sound particularly threatening. He looked like he had been a prize fighter at one time. He had big hands, big shoulders, and a face filled with scar tissue. I estimated him to be about 6'8", in contrast to his buddy who was maybe 5'8". The big guy had dark eyebrows and color in his rugged face. The little guy was an anemic-looking redhead, with thin lips. The big guy was over fifty-years-old. The little guy was in his mid-thirties. They both wore black suits and black ties.

"Why did he want to hire you? How come he thought it necessary?"

The man with the wounded shoulder was not in the room. Another foreign-looking type, with a cigarette holder and smoking cigarette, was standing off to the side of the room and listening to every word as the two thugs looked down at me on the wooden chair they had shoved me onto. The smaller guy pointed a .45, which was a little unusual, since most guys preferred the smaller, easier-to-handle-and-conceal .38. A .45 was O.K. for military use, but for civilian-plug-somebody, a .38 made more sense.

"Her sister and her dad had been killed—wouldn't you think she needed protection?"

"What do you know about their murders?"

"Not much, just what I read in the papers."

"Know anything about why anybody would want to kill them?"

"No. As I said, I was just hired to protect Audrey. That's why I'm here. If I would have been doing my job better, we wouldn't be having this little chat."

The grilling went on for another ten or fifteen minutes until the foreigner, who had been chain-smoking from the cigarette holder, left the room. The questioning stopped and the guy I had winged in the shoulder came in.

"He knows nothing. Dispose of him for the fee you charge."

I didn't like the sound of that, but before I had a chance to object, the anemic-looking guy with the .45 moved around and slugged me from behind with the butt of it. I abruptly departed the realm of consciousness.

Six

When I awoke I was bound, gagged, blindfolded, and lying in the back seat of a moving car. I could hear the motor running and a shift of gears as we climbed a hill that didn't have much of an incline. The car sounded and felt like a pre-war Buick but I couldn't be sure. Buicks had a type of rumbling whine to their engines when you shifted to a lower gear. They pulled well on hills and had a comfortable ride, but they didn't really have a quick getaway like a Ford or Mercury.

As the road curved and descended some before sharply curving and starting to climb again, I knew where we were. The shape of the road told me we had just started up the Hogback. They were taking me where they had killed Irene.

They were probably going to kill me in the same way they had killed her, which meant strangling me. They were hired, professional killers. They had a particular way they operated. They had killed Irene and now they were going to kill me. For them, it was strictly business, probably about five thousand dollars a pop, which was what a good professional killing could command on the open market.

My mind searched for a way out. I knew how they were going to do it, so I didn't have to worry about being shot— unless I tried to escape. To strangle me, they had to get close enough to do it. My hands were tied behind my back. I could only hope they would untie my feet when they took me out of the car. If I had lazy killers who didn't want to carry me, who made me walk to where the body was to be found, I might have a slight chance. At least, my feet would be free and I might be able to do something with them.

The car stopped and I figured we were near the top of the Hogback. I only hoped we weren't all the way up to Lovers' Point. If I jumped off there, the fall would kill me. A little further down and I might have a chance. I waited to either be strangled or have me feet untied.

"Hey, private dick, you conscious now?" It was the voice of the big thug.

I nodded my head vigorously. I wanted them to know I was alive and well enough to walk.

"O.K., we're going to untie your feet and take a little walk. Nothing to worry about, just a little stroll and we're going to let you go." If I believed that, I still believed in Santa Clause and the Easter Bunny.

I could hear the other guy start to laugh, but he tried to stop the laugh from forming, so it came out in a snicker.

My feet were free. Big, powerful hands pulled me from the car.

"Shove him back in,'" the voice I hadn't heard barked. "'Don't let the lights of that car see him."

I was thrown back into the back seat. Lying face down on the seat I heard a car pass. Then I was pulled from the car and onto my feet again, with my back leaning up against the car.

"You're O.K., private dick," the voice of the big thug said. "You know when not to get cute. I thought you might have tried something when that car passed. Then I would have to shoot you."

The other guy snickered. "Come on, let's get it over."

"No, I mean it. This guy's O.K. Did you see the way he took the questioning? No fear. I can tell when they are afraid. He just gave us the answers. Some guys would have made us beat it out of them or been so afraid they would have dribbled all over themselves. This guy's got guts."

I didn't wait for anymore compliments or small talk. When the big guy put his paw on my shoulder to make me walk, I kneed him in the groin with all my strength. I lowered my head in the direction from where I had heard the other voice and charged. My blind aim was good and I hit him in the chest, snapping my head up into his chin as hard as I could. I ran across what I hoped was the road and the drop-off over the side.

A shot rang out just as my running legs propelled me into space and I felt myself falling. My body hit bushes and rocks as I fell and rolled. I couldn't even protect my face because my hands were painfully tied behind me.

When I finally stopped I was barely conscious, but I knew enough to lie dead still. I could hear voices in the distance above

"Do you see him?" the voice of the smaller guy asked.

"Nah, I can't see a thing. The idiot is probably dead. If my shot didn't get him, the fall probably killed him. Taking that leap, didn't that prove what I said about him having guts?"

"Maybe he didn't fall that far."

"It's too dark to see much down there. You see anything?"
"No."

"Well, he had to fall at least twenty or thirty feet, probably farther. If he's not dead, he deserves to live. Guys who ain't afraid to answer the bell deserve to live."

"We could drive back down the road and try to walk in

from the side," the smaller voice suggested.

"It's not worth it." We get our money anyway. If he's not dead, who will ever know? They leave at midnight on the train with the girl and we're out of it. We won't see Klaus again. Who cares if this guy lives, just so long as they don't know he's alive tonight. I don't like working for them damn foreigners anyway."

"They pay good."

"Hey, buddy!" The big voice carried through the vacant summer-night air; it was almost as loud as if he were yelling right next to me. "If you're alive and you hear me, I'm giving you a break because I like you. I shouldn't because my friend's lip is bleeding and I don't feel so good where you kneed me; that wasn't nice. Keep your mouth shut and we'll all come out O.K. If the people we are working for find out you're alive, we'll have to come back and kill you. Then maybe we'll make you feel not so good. Can you hear me?"

Both the blindfold and the gag had been ripped off during my fall, but I said nothing, continuing to lie as still as a dead rabbit on the road. I didn't even look up to where they were. I hoped the bushes, rocks, darkness and silence of the night were sufficient to hide me from the thundering voice blasting into the night air.

After a couple of minutes of silence I heard car doors shut and a car engine start. It still sounded like a Buick. I heard the gears shift as the car went forward and backward, turning around, and then drove off. My body ached all over and I wanted sleep, but I knew I had to get out of there. I had to stop the foreigners from taking Audrey away on the train.

Seven

It took over a half hour to work my way back to the bottom of the Hogback. The hard part was going the rest of the way down the drop-off, slipping and sliding with my hands tied behind me, banging my backside on rock and dirt, catching myself on bushes with my knees or tied hands when I could. At the bottom of the drop-off, I walked on almost level ground to the point where the road started up the Hogback.

I looked a mess when I stood in the road. I was lucky the kids stopped for me. Another car had swerved around me and driven on during my twenty- or thirty-minute stand in the middle of the road. When the kids finally stopped, I was swaying on my feet.

"Who are you, mister?" the teenage boy called as he stood

outside the car on the driver's side and shined the round, chrome spotlight he had mounted on the top part of the door. The beam of light glared into my eyes. Hearing a human voice helped to rejuvenate me.

"I just fell over the side, up the road a bit. I need a lift back into town."

I heard a girl's voice from inside the car say, "Be careful, Bobby."

"Put your hands up in the air where I can see them."

That presented a problem; they were still tied behind my back. "What's your name, kid?" I asked, trying to think of something to say that wouldn't frighten him.

"Don't you worry about my name. You just put your hands in the air where I can see them."

"Maybe he's from one of those flying saucers or something. Don't trust him, Bobby."

"No, I'm not from a flying saucer. I'm a private detective. I was working on a case. Some guys tried to bump me off. I jumped off the side of the road to get away. There, you have it. That's the truth."

"He's crazy, Bobby; that's what he is. Let's get out of here."

"No, wait. Maybe he's telling the truth. Put your hands up in the air so I can see them."

"That's just it, kid. I can't. They're tied behind me. The guys who were going to kill me tied me up so that I couldn't get away. I'm going to turn my back to you and you can shine your light on my hands. O.K.?"

"Don't do it, Bobby. He's from outer space or a convict or something. Let's get out of here."

"Oh, shut it, Barbara. Let me see his hands."

"You're not taking me to Lovers' Point tonight. Talk to me like that, and you can take me home right now. You're not making out with me tonight."

I could see that I was in danger of losing my ride. Sex is, in my opinion, a more powerful force than altruism or whatever they call it when somebody does a good deed. I tried something that, at times, could be more powerful than sex.

"Bobby, I'll give you twenty bucks if you take me back into town. Your girl is right; I could be anything. But I'm not. I'm a private eye and I've got to get back to town to save a woman who has been kidnapped."

"Oh brother, Bobby, if you'll believe that, you'll believe anything. I think this guy's a nut case. He belongs in the booby hatch."

"Ah, the wisdom of the young," I said, trying to control my temper. "The offer has just gone up to forty bucks, kid, and that's my top dollar. You can buy you and Barbara about eighty malted milks for that. That's about 200 gallons of gas. Come on, kid, for all that loot, isn't it worth a little risk to take me back to town? Once you've got all that money, Barbara will love you forever."

"This guy's a real jerk. My love has nothing to do with how much money you have, Bobby."

I shut up, deciding there was no reasoning with the teenage mind. It was quiet for a minute and then Bobby said, "O.K., I'm taking you to town, but I want to see your money first."

"Nothing doing, kid, I wasn't born yesterday. You take my money and leave me out here while you and your girlfriend ride around drinking malted milks. You deposit me at Galliger's car lot on West Colfax and then I'll give you the money. Joe's closed the lot and is probably asleep by now, but if you think it's necessary, we'll wake him up so that he can vouch for me."

"How come you want to go to the car lot?" Bobby asked.

"'Good question, kid. You might become a detective someday. You'll see my office there. It's not much, but it's got my name on the door. I can make a call I've got to make and get some money out of my office safe to replace the forty bucks you're going to take out of my wallet. And since the bad guys took the car I was driving earlier in the day, I'll be able to pull another one off Galliger's car lot to use when I go after the lady I'm trying to get back from the bad guys."

"Can I go with you, I mean when you go after the bad guys?"

"'Bobby!'"

"Kid, you're O.K., but you've got to learn to not let dames rule your life, which is pretty hard to do. No, you can't go with me, but if we don't get going, I'm not going to be able to catch the bad guys."

I saw the lights of an approaching car. "Well, kid, how about it? You want my forty bucks or shall I make my offer to the next guy?"

Bobby helped me into the back seat of his four-door, 1936, brown Plymouth. I started to ask him to untie my hands, but I didn't because I didn't want to have to explain to Barbara for thirty minutes why it would be safe to untie me.

"Galliger's car lot on West Colfax, kid. It's close to Sheridan." I lay down on the seat and took what seemed like the shortest nap of my life.

Barbara insisted on waking up Joe Galliger to verify my trustworthiness before they untied me. Joe, coming to the door in red pajamas and without his stub of a cigar, hardly looked like the usual Joe.

"Marty, what the hell happened to you? You look like you have been through the Second World War."

"I went through it, remember. Tell these kids I'm O.K., so they'll untie me."

"Two kids tied you up. Jeez, Marty, you're losing your touch."

"No, Joe, they didn't tie me up, but it's been that kind of a day. Tell them I'm O.K. and to untie me."

"Yeah, kids, he's O.K. Kind of a careless bum sometimes, but O.K. Untie him. Where's the '41 Merc, Marty?"

Bobby started untying me.

"I'll report it stolen, Joe. I figure you'll get it back without any damage. They didn't want the car, they wanted me."

I rubbed my hands together in front of me. "That feels good. The rest of me feels painfully dead, but at least my wrists can come back to life from those rope burns. That must have been some knot they tied. What was it like, kid?"

"Square knot. I learned it in Scouts."

"Oh," I said, a little embarrassed.

"Jeez, Marty, you can't even get out of a square knot. Besides, if it's painful, how can you be dead? Nobody can be painfully dead. You're either painful or dead."

"Can it, Joe. My patience is a little short tonight. Give me something to drive to Union Station. I've got a train to catch. You can either pick up the car or leave it there until I get back."

"Not another car, Marty. You get my cream puff '41 Merc stolen, and then you want another car."

"Have it ready in fifteen minutes. A lady's life may depend on it. I'll tell you all about it when I get back. I'll report the Merc stolen when I call Harry Makris as soon as I wash my face. Let me use your bathroom to clean up. I need a quick shave. I've got some clean clothes hanging in my office. I'd go back to the Pig and Poke and clean up in my room, but there's not time."

I started for Joe's bathroom. We were standing in the living room of his little frame house that was on the side of his car lot, next to the little office I rented off to the side of his house.

"Aren't you forgetting something?" Bobby almost yelled at me.

"Yeah, kid, here's twenty. Joe, give the kid twenty. I'll get it back for you out of my office safe."

"See, I told you that you shouldn't have trusted him, Bobby. He didn't even have the forty dollars on him when he promised you the money. Bobby, you need to be more careful."

"No offense, kid, but a dame like this will make an old man out of you before your time. Get yourself a doll that lets you breathe a little."

"Or stay single like me," Joe put in quickly. "How do you think I managed to buy my own car lot? I didn't spend it on women and I saved my money when I was just a car salesman."

"You couldn't get a woman in those red pajamas if you tried," I said, allowing myself a hint of a smile for the first time in many hours. "Really, Joe, you ought to be ashamed of yourself, letting these kids see you in something like that. What do you think it is, hunting season?"

I didn't wait for a reply. I could see Barbara getting ready to flare up at the suggestion I had made to Bobby about getting a new girlfriend. Maybe I had done somebody some good today, even though I had lost Audrey to the kidnappers.

Eight

I was buttoning up my clean white shirt, having a bourbon and water, and had my feet propped up on my desk while I was telling Harry Makris over the telephone what to do. It was five minutes after eleven and he had just gone to bed before I called. I could hear his wife rolling on the bed beside him.

"Yeah, Harry, if you get somebody over to the house where they grilled me, you may still catch them or pick up some clues on them. You might get lucky and still find Audrey there...

"Harry, they've killed twice and I don't think cop-killing is something they would shy away from. Klaus is no slouch, so tell your boys to be extra careful...

"Yeah, that's right. One of the guys is called Klaus. I think he's the one I winged in the shoulder. He seemed like the boss of the outfit to me. Seemed German, but that's what you would expect with a name like Klaus. If you find a black '41 Mercury coupe, it belongs to Galliger. That's what I was driving when they snatched the girl and me...

"Yes, Harry, Klaus made me drive it and him to the house...

"No, Harry, I'm not losing my touch. It's just been that kind of a day. Look, Harry, I've got to go...

"Oh, maybe I'll nose around a little. Then again, maybe I'll just hit the sack or have a drink at the Red Horse. I'm awful tired and sore...

"I'm sore because I got slugged twice and fell down a rock pile later. I'll tell you about it when I see you. Get moving and you may pick up Klaus before he moves the girl."

I stood, hung up the telephone, stuffed the clean white shirttail into my clean blue trousers, and pulled my spare .38 out of the safe along with enough money for a ticket to wherever I might have to go. I put on the blue-and-white-checked sports coat that went with the blue trousers. I stuffed a blue, wide floral tie into the left side pocket of the sports coat. I didn't plan on wearing it, but sometimes a tie comes in handy.

I purposely had not told Harry about the girl being taken on the train at midnight. The police would show up in force. Without any time to plan a move, they would probably bust in like gangbusters, which is what cops do for a living. In the commotion they might either lose Audrey or get her killed. Taking my time to retrieve her, I figured I could do it safely and professionally, without losing Audrey or information. Besides, I wouldn't mind dealing with Klaus myself. We had a few scores to settle.

I had to hurry to arrive at the train depot by 11:30. I wanted to give myself enough time to allow for time before or after midnight. I had heard the big thug say they were leaving with the girl at midnight. That could be before or after midnight, but which direction and which train? I needed to study the sched-ules and buy my ticket. If luck was on my side, I would be able to see them boarding the train with Audrey.

To Kansas City, leaving on track five at 12:10 A.M. How could I be sure? The only other train leaving near midnight was going west. I decided Europeans would be going east. If I would have been pursuing Orientals, I would have gone west.

I bought a ticket for Kansas City and then sat at the L-shaped counter in the coffee shop, having a cup of coffee and a ham sandwich. I thought that was a good place to look inconspicuous and keep an eye on the cavernous waiting room. Practically everybody passed by the coffee shop on the way to and from the boarding areas. I had a clear view through the plate glass window at the bottom of the L.

I was about three-quarters of the way through the ham sandwich when I saw them. I picked up the *Rocky Mountain News* on the counter by me and dropped a dollar bill on the counter.

"Here, Miss, this is for my sandwich and coffee. I'm taking this paper too."

"Don't you want your change?" the counter lady called after me.

"It's yours." After she took out for the sandwich, coffee, and newspaper, there would be fifteen or twenty cents left over. I figured I was the last of the red-hot tippers.

It was just the foreigners who were with Audrey. I was glad the big thug and his smaller pal hadn't come along. It was Klaus and the chain-smoking, weasel-looking guy with the cigarette holder who was about the same age as Klaus— maybe fifty. Chain-smoking weasel face had a small, black mustache like my own. I decided right then that I would shave mine off the first chance I got.

Audrey looked straight ahead as she walked between the two of them. She was still wearing the same clothes she had been snatched in—navy-blue pleated skirt, white blouse, black flats with no stockings. The foreigners were wearing suits. Klaus was in dark brown and his accomplice was wearing light gray.

I felt sorry for the poor kid. She must have felt awful after all she had been through, but she was still holding up with a steady look of being able to take it.

We boarded the train without incident. There were maybe fifty people getting on the train and it was easy to keep myself far enough back in the crowd to avoid detection by the kidnappers. My casual interest in the newspaper I had taken from the counter of the coffee shop was of some benefit, because it was easy to be looking down at the sports page while waiting at the boarding area.

I had purchased a ticket for a sleeping compartment. I didn't want my face seen more than it had to be. Furthermore, when I got Audrey away from the kidnappers, I might need someplace to safely stash her unless I was lucky enough to totally eliminate Klaus and his partner.

I didn't inform the train detective for the same reason I hadn't informed Harry and the police department. I didn't want anybody rushing in and getting Audrey killed.

Locating Audrey and the kidnappers was not too difficult. They had a compartment on the same car as I did. My sleeping compartment was at one end of the car, theirs was at the other. Mine was at the end next to the dining car. Theirs was at the back end, with two more passenger cars behind them. Since this was a streamliner passenger train, there was no caboose at the end as on freight trains.

After carefully checking out the surrounding cars, having to dart into the dining car at one point to avoid detection by the weasel, my mind began to work on what was the best way to rescue Audrey safely. I doubted they would ever bring her out of their compartment. If they gave her any food, they would probably take it in to her. This meant that one of them would stay with her while the other went to the dining car to eat or bring back food to Audrey or the other one. I figured they would go for food. They didn't appear to be into self-denial.

It seemed almost too simple to grab the first one. All I would have to do was to grab him as he went by my compartment on the way to or from the dining car. The second one would be the problem. He probably wouldn't open the compartment until the first returned. If I snatched the first, there would be no return.

I could force the first to go back to the compartment at gun point. Then when he got the other guy to open the compartment, I could rush in. Too much risk of shooting with Audrey in the line of fire, not a good plan.

It was the weasel who came out first. I had my compartment door open about six inches and was sitting on the bench seat at an angle where I could see if someone passed by in the direction of the dining car. My .38 rested on the seat beside me.

Weasel moved too fast for me to grab him on the way to the dining car, which had not been my plan anyway. I wanted him coming toward me instead of away from me. I saw his back vanish into the dining car, and it was twenty-three minutes before he came out again.

They had decided to feed Audrey. A brown paper sack was in his hand. Klaus would be accustomed to better. If his junior partner ate in the dining car and came back safely, then Klaus would not forgo the pleasure of good dining.

As the weasel stepped in front of my view, I stepped out. "Easy, pal, or I blow a hole in you," I said quietly.

He looked down at the .38 I had shoved into his belly.

"Now, if you'll just step into my compartment, I'll relieve you of that brown bag you are carrying."

"It is only food," he wheezed out in his strong German accent.

"I know, but maybe I'm hungry."

I slugged him on the back of the head with my gun butt when I followed him into the compartment. My arms caught him as he slumped. I kicked the door shut with my right heel. I wanted him alive, but out of commission while I dealt with Klaus, and I didn't want to have to worry about him.

I laid him on the bench seat, facing the seat back. I tied his hands behind his back with the tie I had in my sports coat pocket. His own gray tie was used to tie his ankles together. My white handkerchief pulled into his mouth and tied tightly in back of his head would allow him to make incoherent sounds, but with the compartment door closed, who would hear him?

I grabbed the back of his belt in my right hand and the back of his shirt and suit-coat collar with my left hand. I lifted him off the seat and laid him on the floor. He wasn't very heavy, so it was an easy lift. I didn't want him rolling off the seat onto the floor and breaking his neck while I was gone.

I was now ready to wait for Klaus. When the weasel didn't return, I figured Klaus would come out of his hole eventually. Sometimes, with a rat, you have to exercise patience. I would wait in the dining car because I knew that would be where he would go to look for the weasel.

Nine

It was an hour and seventeen minutes before Klaus came into the dining car. He was a careful one, waiting that long. He did not bring Audrey with him, which led me to wonder about her safety.

I still had the same newspaper that I had read at least three times. I pulled it up to my face once again as I saw him enter. My seat was close to the entrance, so he did not have to go far before coming by my table. At 2:21 A.M. the dining car was nearly deserted. They kept it open for night owls who might require a late-night snack or be in need of someplace to drink coffee when they no longer wished to fight insomnia. Two of us were drinking coffee and reading at opposite ends of the car and a third guy in the middle was having something to eat. At this hour, there was only one attendant on duty in the dining car, and he was busying himself behind the counter, wiping water glasses with a white dish towel. My greeting to Klaus did not attract any attention other than a quick glance from the others in the dining car.

"Klaus, so good of you to come," I said quietly, getting up from my chair and shielding the pistol in my right hand with the newspaper in my left hand. Klaus could see the .38, but the others couldn't.

"I thought you were dead," Klaus said, with only a limited amount of surprise.

"Come now, Klaus, it hasn't been that long since we saw each other. Let's go to your compartment and talk over old times. How is that shoulder of yours? I suppose it's bandaged under your shirt. I hope you don't need a bandage for the other one, but next time, you probably won't need a bandage at all."

Klaus turned and I followed him out of the dining car.

"No, not this one," I said when Klaus stopped at a compartment that was not his own. "I prefer your own compartment."

Klaus said nothing and moved down the gently swaying, well-lighted train corridor to his own compartment, where he stopped. We stood for a moment, with the only sound being the iron train wheels rolling on the iron tracks, making their kackity-klack rumble.

"Let's not be reluctant; unlock the door and open it, Klaus. You seem to be just a little hesitant about this whole thing. Where is that vaunted German efficiency? Heil, Hitler, Klaus! Does that get you moving faster?"

He turned his head and his eyes flashed in anger at me.

"Go ahead, Klaus. Nothing would give me more pleasure than to take care of you right here. My time in the war was spent in the Pacific, but I'm not adverse to killing Germans."

"There is no need for that," Klaus said in his heavy German accent, turning his head back toward the compartment door. "I'll unlock the door." He started to reach into his left trouser pocket.

"Hold it!"

He stopped.

"Put your hands above you on the door."

He complied as best he could, having trouble raising his right arm because of the shoulder wound. I used my left hand to pat him down. He winced when I tapped the area near his shoulder bandage. I located his pistol in a shoulder holster on the opposite side, carried under his arm.

When I had him turn around and I reached to remove the pistol, I thought he might make a move. That was a chance for escape, but it wouldn't have done any good because I would have planted a bullet in his heart. Maybe he knew that, because he didn't do anything except stand there with his hands in the air.

"A German Lugar, it doesn't surprise me, Klaus. What's this, the pistol you carried in the war? Probably a German officer, right?"

He nodded his head.

"O.K., turn around, drop your hands, and let's get this door open."

Klaus retrieved a key out of his left trouser pocket and unlocked the door. When it swung open, I got careless. I was trying to hold the German Lugar and my own .38, see into the compartment, and keep an eye on Klaus—all at the same time. The train porter distracted me further by appearing from the dining car and staring at us. I should have been able to handle all of that, but Klaus' failure to try anything when I had removed his gun made me a little complacent.

I never expected a blow to come from his right elbow, but never underestimate the dedication of a German officer. It must have pained his right shoulder tremendously to swing the right elbow back at me, but it was effective. As he cried out in pain, my gun and the German Lugar fell to the floor. Klaus was running into the next car by the time I started after him.

For Klaus, there was no place to go. I caught him just before we stumbled out onto the platform at the end of the train. We fell back onto the railing, both of us nearly falling off into the darkness of night.

Klaus came around with a knee to my groin as I wrapped my left arm around the back of his neck and laid my right forearm across his throat. He struggled as the wind went out of him and I heard him gurgle as he felt the force of my arm. I could see panic in his eyes, much like a frightened animal ready to die.

I could have thrown him from the platform of the speeding train and let the fall onto the railroad tracks kill him. I could have held him a minute longer and let him die in my arms. I did neither. I released the pressure of my forearm so that he could breathe and then I kneed him in the groin. With Klaus doubled over in pain and gasping for air, he stumbled back to the compartment with me dragging him by the collar.

I made sure Klaus did not get near either of the pistols I had dropped. I picked up mine and used my foot to shove the Lugar into the compartment. Klaus was pretty meek as I dragged him into the compartment.

Audrey was tied on the bench seat, much as I had tied the weasel. Her face and body were facing outward. She was breathing, but unconscious.

"What have you done to her?" I demanded.

"It is nothing, a sedative, that is all. She will sleep for awhile and be perfectly all right." Klaus stood up nearly straight and began to gain back some of his composure. "All of us Germans are not barbaric."

"Is that why you killed Irene Hampton, because you're not barbaric?"

"I didn't kill her."

"No? You hired those two thugs who tried to kill me, and had them do it."

"I hired them, but not to kill Professor Berkowitz or his daughters. I wanted to protect them. Somebody else was killing them. My government wanted them alive because of the professor's knowledge of, shall we say, certain things. I was sent to kidnap them and take them back to East Berlin. I have told you more than I should have, but I want you to know that I am not responsible for Professor Berkowitz's death or the death of any of his family."

The surprise at this lie or truth did not have time to sink in before a voice behind me said, "Don't make a move with that gun, mister, or you're dead."

I froze.

"O.K., drop it and nobody gets hurt."

I dropped the .38, half-expecting the fall and the jarring of the weapon to cause it to discharge. It retained all of its bullets when it hit the floor.

"Both of you, get your hands up in the air and turn around."

I complied. Klaus could raise his right hand only a little above his shoulder. Pain was written all over his face. The man holding the revolver was a beefy baldheaded guy in a sloppy gray suit and yellow tie that didn't go with the suit.

"I said for both of you to get your hands in the air."

"He can't," I volunteered. "I put a slug in his shoulder earlier. It looks like he's bleeding pretty bad again."

"Who are you and what is going on here?"

"I'm a private detective and I'm stopping this man from kidnapping this woman. You must be the train dick. Who else shows up when you don't need him?"

The porter stepped up behind the man holding the gun. Both of them were standing in the aisle, looking into the small compartment.

"He is the train detective and I called him when I saw something going on."

"O.K.," I said wearily, "I'll get it all sorted out for you, and you can wire ahead to the Kansas City Police Department to be expecting us when we arrive. Have you got a doctor on board? He said she had a sedative. We need to check it out and make sure it is not more serious. "

"Just a sedative, that is all," Klaus said as he fell toward the train detective and the porter. The porter partially caught him and cushioned his fall. It was not a trick; exertion and loss of blood had caused him to collapse.

"Let me untie the lady while you look after him. I'm not going anyplace."

The train detective nodded his consent. I started to untie the beautiful figure of Audrey while the train detective rolled the bleeding figure of Klaus over on his back and tried to undo his dark brown suit coat, tie and white shirt to stem the flow of blood from the wound. The porter went in search of a doctor.

"Hey, this guy's not going to make it," the train detective said to me from his kneeling position. "His heart just stopped."

"Well, give him artificial respiration," I said, having finished untying Audrey's ankles. Her hands were still tied behind her back and she was sleeping soundly.

"I can't. It'll just make him lose more blood if I roll him over and pump his back."

"Yeah, I guess you're right," I said as I reached down and started to slap Klaus' face lightly and then harder. "Klaus, Klaus, wake up! Klaus! Klaus!"

Klaus did not respond, and I knew that another of Hitler's reportedly superhuman, racially-superior beings had become all-too mortal. I figured I still had the weasel for information if I could get it out of him.

"He's done, pal," I said as I went back to the task of untying Audrey. I had to get behind her back to untie her hands, and trying to be as gentle as I could, her body seemed all-too close to mine.

The doctor, looking as though he had just gotten out of bed and thrown on his trousers and shirt, arrived before I completed the task of untying her. He tried to revive Klaus with a shot in the arm of something from his black medical bag. It did no good, and he turned his attention to Audrey.

"Yes, it just appears to be a sedative," he said after listening, poking, and feeling around that beautiful sleeping body for a few minutes. "She'll probably sleep a few more hours, depending on the strength of what she was given. She should be watched for any complication while she is asleep. Call me if she experiences anything unusual or you need my help."

He turned and started to leave the compartment. "I can't

even get a good night's sleep on the train. Why do you think I took this trip? To get away from patients, that's why."

I stepped out and watched the doctor go up the lightly swaying aisle toward the dining car as the porter came down the aisle. I saw that my compartment door was ajar. I started to move up the aisle.

"Hold it!" the train detective said to me. "Where do you think you're going?"

I glanced around and saw that he was holding his gun on me.

"I found another person kidnapped," the porter said. "I untied him and he's on his way down here."

The weasel came out of the compartment, but instead of coming toward us, brushed by the doctor and headed into the dining car.

"He's getting away. Put that gun down and let me go after him."

"A kidnapper you mean?" the train detective asked.

"Yes, a kidnapper," I said in exasperation.

"Wait here," the train detective said as he brushed beside me and started after the weasel who could no longer be seen. I didn't wait, but followed at a distance, hoping my jumpy train detective wouldn't get overly excited and shoot me.

After chasing the weasel through five cars, the weasel could go no further because of the engine. Instead of surrendering, he climbed the ladder up onto the top of the train. The train detective followed. I was thinking, 'Don't shoot him,' just before I heard the shots.

The train detective nearly slipped on the ladder as he came down. His hands were shaking as he pointed the pistol at me. He was breathing hard and sweating profusely.

"I could have run away. I'm here. Put that damn thing down."

The train detective lowered the pistol. "Yeah, I guess you're right. You could have run, but you didn't."

"Did you hit him?" I asked.

"I think so, but either way, he fell off the train, he's dead.

You don't fall off a train at this speed and live."

"Thanks, pal. There goes my other source of information as to why they kidnapped the woman you let me untie. Always nice to have a train dick around when you don't need one. Maybe you can come to Denver sometime and I'll do you the same favor."

The train detective was annoyed at my remarks, but he was too shaky over the chase and the shooting to mumble anything other than, "I did what I had to do."

After giving the train detective a rough sketch of the kidnapping and telling him to wire the K.C. police and the Denver police, I was given charge of Audrey. The train detective let me carry her in my arms to my compartment as he followed. He and the porter would take care of the body of Klaus, after which, he said he was going to have a stiff drink. "You want me to have the porter bring you one?" he asked.

"Yeah, thanks, pal, bourbon and water. I guess we've both had a night of it. Sorry about what I said about you shooting that guy. I wanted him alive so that he could tell me what was going on with the kidnapping. We both did what we had to. You did O.K. The bad guy didn't get away, and that's what you're here for."

He looked appreciatively at me. "I'll have the porter send the bourbon and water."

As we rolled through the night to K.C., I sipped the bourbon and water and looked at Audrey resting peacefully with a pillow under her head. Her feet were propped up on my lap as we sat on the bench seat. I decided it hadn't been too bad of a night after all. I had got the innocent back safely. The bad guys had taken the deep six and I was alone with a beautiful woman, having a bourbon and water. Too bad she wasn't awake to enjoy my company.

On the way back from K.C., she was awake, and she was most appreciative. The railroad had provided us both with sleeping compartments, free of charge, after they had heard the story of the kidnapping from the railroad detective. They could have saved money on Audrey's compartment. She spent practically the entire return trip in my compartment.

Ten

When we arrived in Denver at 1:37 A.M., Harry Makris, two uniformed police officers, and Barry Hampton were waiting for us. The two uniformed police officers were to keep the crowd of reporters and about a hundred fire-chasing onlookers under control.

"What's all this?" I asked Harry as Audrey and I blinked into the popping flash bulbs.

"The K.C. police and the train dick gave out with the story. I tried to keep it under wraps. You and Audrey are front-page news. Why didn't you let me know you were going after her?"

"You covered the house; I covered the train. They left the house before you could grab them. I was your back-up. Anything at the house?"

"No, it was clean. We did retrieve the '41 Mercury for Galliger. You know, Marty, sometimes you've got the makings of a real good cop. How about joining the force sometime?"

"Not a chance," I said as I watched Barry Hampton take Audrey in his arms and kiss her. For a brother-in-law, welcome-home kiss, it was a little too passionate. I didn't like him planting his lips on hers.

My disapproval didn't have time to fester as Hampton turned to me. "Good work, Mayfield! Good work, Mayfield!" He was pumping my hand, smiling, and patting me on the back.

Flash bulbs were continuing to pop and the two cops were having a hard time holding the crowd back. I could hear one of them saying, "Official police business. You'll get your chance in a few minutes as soon as Detective Makris gives us the O.K."

The promise of getting at us soon restrained them, but it didn't stop the flash bulbs. I wondered why they needed fifty million pictures of us. I knew there had to be more than just the *Rocky Mountain News* and the *Denver Post* covering the story. As I was to learn later, the national wire services had picked up the story, and magazines, as well as newspapers, were covering us. I didn't think it was all that big of a deal, but they did. The idea of foreign agents from behind the Iron Curtain kidnapping an American citizen was enough to send the press into a frenzy.

I didn't give anybody the story that Klaus had given me, not even Harry. Everybody thought the case was over except for catching the hired thugs. Harry told the reporters that we suspected international espionage over uranium. The foreign agents had died at Red Rocks Park and on the train, thanks to the efforts of private detective Martin Mayfield and train detective James Scheeley. The two thugs, hired by the foreign agents to kill Irene and her father, were still at large. The Denver Police Department and the F.B.I., since espionage appeared to be involved, would not cease in their efforts until the thugs were apprehended. The kidnapping of Audrey and taking her across state lines also made it a federal crime.

Barry Hampton paid me the remaining four thousand of the five thousand and thanked me profusely when I accepted the check from him the next day in front of his downtown bank. Reporters were gathered around, snapping pictures as I accepted the check. They were probably tipped off by Hampton or Audrey, who was also present. Then again, maybe it was that I couldn't go anyplace without reporters dogging my movements.

The reporters called for Audrey to give me a kiss of appreciation, which she did. This time, it was Hampton's turn to do the slow burn while Audrey paid me in full with a kiss that caused the reporters to hoot and whistle.

With the exception of getting to know Audrey, I wished I could slip back into the quiet life I had before the whole episode came up. I didn't mind being kissed by her in front of the cameras, but the rest of it would be better if it never happened. For a couple of weeks I couldn't even drink bourbon and water in the Red Horse without having somebody ask me about the whole thing.

When the pictures were taken, I still had the mustache. I shaved it off as soon as things quieted down a little. It didn't completely change my appearance, but it helped a little. I needed less notoriety and more anonymity to continue my own search for the thugs.

I knew they were the bridge to who had really hired them to do the killings, assuming that Klaus had told me the truth, which he may not have. If he hadn't told me the truth, it had died with him, but the truth was still alive with the two thugs, wherever they were hiding. They were lying low because the heat was on. Every police department in the country had Audrey's and my description of them. They weren't likely to be found quickly or easily.

Eleven

It was at the Pig and Poke that I got my best clue as to where the thugs might be. Frank Brodrick, torn between loyalty to an ex-fighter and to me and law and order, finally told me who he thought the big guy might be. I reasoned that if the big guy was an ex-pug, Frank might have a line on him. It took two days of me jogging Frank's memory with questions about fighters to finally get him to come around. Frank called me over to a booth and sat across from me with a cup of black coffee in front of him. His big hands wrapped around the coffee cup as if it were the size of a peanut. He still had the look of a fighter, middle-aged and a little out-of-shape, but still tough.

"You want some coffee or something, Marty?"

"Just information from your memory, Frank. You figure

out yet who the big guy might be?"

"Yeah, Marty, I figured it out. I thought when I read the description they gave in the papers a couple of weeks ago that I might know who it was. I didn't want to point the finger unjustly, so I checked around a little. It's Bobo, the Heart. We called him 'the Heart' because he didn't like to hurt guys too bad in the ring. He'd finish them off, but he wouldn't hurt them more than he had to."

Frank snapped his fingers at Ida, the waitress. "Bring me some toast to go with this coffee, honey; I'm a little hungry. You sure you don't want something, Marty?"

I shook my head "no."

"Well, Marty, I heard he went sour, but I never thought he had the stomach for hired killing."

"Life does strange things to people, Frank. Sometimes people go sour. Sometimes they reform and go clean. You just never know."

"Some of the guys tell me Bobo went sour, and that he's been doing strong-arm stuff for hire. I saw him in here less than a month ago. Said he was just drifting through to the West Coast. Looks like he dropped off and did a little killing on the way."

"You think he's on the West Coast, Frank?"

"Unless he stopped off in his hometown of Leadville. Bobo was from a mining family. Jack Dempsey was doing fights in bars for money; that's before he became a big-name fighter. He was fighting under the name of, I think, "Kid Blackie." He flattened Bobo, but he remembered him. When Dempsey became big-time, he needed sparring partners and gave Bobo a job. Bobo went on to a fight career of his own, but he was never really a contender. Bobo's still a celebrity in his hometown. They probably wouldn't shield him from the law, but it might be hard for them to turn him in. Small towns are like that. I figure he probably isn't in Leadville or he would have been caught by now. He might have gone on to the West Coast. If you want to lose yourself in a crowd, the West Coast beats Leadville."

"Where on the West Coast?"

"There's a gym in L.A. where a lot of ex-pugs hang out, kind of an old folks' home for ex-fighters. They punch the bag, swap lies about their fighting days and pretend they're still fighters. They still get to give young fighters advice. It's called Ryan's Gym. I don't think Bobo is going to hang around the place with all the heat that is on him, but I think somebody will know something about where he is. You lay down fifty bucks for information and it might get you some leads on his whereabouts."

"How about Bobo's sidekick?"

"Small-time hood from back east." Frank started to butter the toast the waitress had just set in front of him. The part in the middle of his combed-straight-back, steel-gray hair was just as straight as the knife. His gray-blue eyes were inexpressive as he talked. Had I not become a friend of his through renting one of his motel rooms, he was the kind of guy I would have steered clear of. I wouldn't have wanted to be on the wrong side of his anger. "Don't know much about him, but that's my guess as to how Bobo got into the business of killing people. Bobo should have stayed with good people. You hang around with bums and it does you no good."

"Anything on the other guy other than he's from back east. Where back east?"

"That's all I heard, Marty. I never saw him from Adam."

"Thanks, Frank. I owe you as usual."

"No, you don't, Marty, and that's unusual. You're all paid up on your rent and your restaurant tab. This case has been good for you." Frank smiled, revealing white teeth that were a little crooked on the top and bottom but in surprisingly good shape, considering his former occupation of professional fighter. He bit into a piece of toast and snapped his fingers for the waitress to bring him more coffee.

"Yeah, that's what being a celebrity does to a guy, Frank."

"Don't blow it all, Marty. I've seen fighters who made millions and had nothing to show for it. It is rumored Joe Lewis may be in financial trouble. Can you imagine that, a guy like Joe Lewis needing dough?"

"How come he retired then?"

"The years are catching up with him. But mark my words, he'll try for a comeback. If the rumors about the money are true, he'll be back to try to pick up a little dough."

"Well, I wouldn't know about that. You're the fight expert."

I turned my head a little and talked softer so that the waitress wouldn't hear what I said in the event that she might have been able to hear. "Frank, I'm going to check out Ryan's Gym in L.A. Get me an address if you can. And, Frank, keep it quiet as to where I've gone. I want a little breathing room from press and people. I think I would just be wasting my time in Leadville, so I'm going to skip it. With all the heat that is on, L.A. sounds like a place where Bobo and his buddy might try to lose themselves. Even there, I think it would be tough for them to go unrecognized."

"What other cases you working on?"

I raised my voice to its normal volume and resumed a normal conversational tone. "None. I think this case kind of spoiled me. I'm going to wait for just the big ones to come along. No more dog-bite cases for me."

"In case the big ones never come along, maybe you had better give me a little advance on your room and your grub, just in case you never make any money again."

"You're really an encouragement, Frank. But maybe you're right. I'll get you five hundred bucks before I go. That should take care of my tab for a long time."

"I didn't mean for you to put up that much, Marty, but it is a good idea. You're not going to become a stumblebum as long as I'm around. When you're punch-drunk or washed up, maybe you'll still have something left if you listen to me."

Thanks, Frank," I said as I stood and left for Joe Galliger's car lot.

I must have been feeling real generous because I also gave Joe Galliger a chunk of money. I gave him three hundred and fifty for the black '41 Mercury coupe with the white side walls that I had decided to drive to California. It had handled real well when I had pursued the kidnappers to Red Rocks Park. I thought that if I ended up in a car race with Bobo and his friend, the '41 Merc was a good car to have. We were sitting in Joe Galliger's office as we did the deal.

"Why are you buying it, Marty? You know you could just borrow it." Joe looked genuinely puzzled at my purchase of the car as he completed the paperwork."

"It wouldn't be right for me to drive it all the way to California and back on just a borrow. That's a little more than my usual distance. If it comes back in O.K. condition, I'll sell it back to you for a couple of hundred. That way I won't be beating the hell out of your pocketbook. If it gets all banged up somewhere, you won't have lost anything."

Joe had me sign a couple of papers I didn't pay much attention to. Then we walked outside to the car.

"Expecting it to be a rough caper, Marty?"

"I hope not, but I can't guarantee it. Just keep your mouth shut about where I've gone."

"You've got it, Marty." He patted the shiny black left front fender of the Merc. "I had the oil changed, got it greased, and had it checked out mechanically for you. You might want to change the oil and have it greased before you come back. You wouldn't want to burn out a bearing or anything. It's still a cream puff."

"Yeah, sure, Joe, a cream puff."

He didn't know I was kidding him, but whether or not it was a cream puff, it made it to Los Angeles in about thirty-seven hours, which was good time. I stopped for coffee, sandwiches, and a little road-side snoozing along the way. In L.A. I checked into a small, modest-priced hotel for some real snoozing and to wash away the road grime I had accumulated.

Twelve

Ryan's Gym wasn't hard to find. I had the address Frank had given me, and if I wouldn't have had the address, I could have looked it up in the telephone book. It was July, hot, and the fighters smelled accordingly.

I was direct in what I wanted. I decided there was no benefit in trying to be evasive about what I was seeking. That might cause them to clam up. With fifty bucks as a standing offer, I thought somebody might give me some information on the whereabouts of Bobo. I hung around the gym for three days without even a nibble.

On the third day, when the gym closed at 9 P.M., I dropped into a bar for a bourbon and water and then drove back to my hotel as usual. As I got out of the Mercury two guys, standing next to a tree by the street, grabbed me. They made no attempt to hide their faces and I could see them in the light from the street lamp. I recognized them as two of the old-time pugs from Ryan's Gym.

Shoving me up against the car, one guy held me while the other guy swung a roundhouse right that connected with my jaw.

My knees buckled, but it didn't put me out. I retaliated with a left elbow in the rib of the guy who was holding me and a kick to the groin of the guy who had swung the right. Both of them doubled over.

I grabbed the guy I had kicked in the groin and slammed his head into the tree. It was lights out for him for a long time as he crumpled to the base of the tree.

The other guy was a little tougher to put down. He managed to lay in a kidney punch as I turned around. I caught him with an overhead right to the nose that knocked him onto the hood of the Merc. He wasn't unconscious as he slid off the hood into a sitting position by the front wheel, but his nose was bleeding profusely and his eyes were glazed. I started to kick him but decided he had had enough.

"You broke my nose," he sputtered as he held his left hand up to the bleeding nose that was limp and bent to the right side of his face. Blood ran all over his hand.

"It probably wasn't the first time," I said as I tossed him the white handkerchief I pulled out of my trouser pocket. "See if you can stop the geyser you've got going before you bleed to death."

His eyes looked frightened as he held the handkerchief against his nose. He was pushing sixty, as was the other guy who was sleeping at the base of the tree. The guy with the broken nose was nearly bald; the other guy had a full head of gray hair.

"Aren't you boys getting a little old for this kind of work?"

"Yeah, maybe," he said while holding his head back, "but we almost took you. It's tough making a living. Social Security won't kick in for a few years and neither Tommy nor me has any income."

"He's Tommy?" I nodded at the guy at the base of the tree.

"Yeah, that's Tommy. In his day he was a real contender. I fought for the title twice myself."

"Who hired you to rough me up?"

"Bobo, the Heart, heard you was asking around about him. He sent word to me and Tommy, along with five hundred bucks to rough you up bad enough that you wouldn't stay on his tail. The five hundred was tough to turn down. I guess we blew it. I guess you're going to turn us over to the cops and then Bobo will be after us too for botching the job."

"Not necessarily. Keep your five hundred and I won't turn you over to the police if you tell me where Bobo is. If I get to him before he comes after you, you won't have to worry about him coming after you. No cops, no Bobo. You and Tommy just made five hundred dollars for scaring me off Bobo's trail. No one ever has to know that you guys didn't take me. Now, where's Bobo?"

"It don't seem right to take his five hundred and then tell you where he is."

"Suit yourself. It's the cops, an assault charge, and Bobo and the guys at Ryan's knowing you botched the job. I'd say you would be smart to tell me where Bobo is."

Tommy groaned as he started to come around.

"Tijuana. There's too much heat on him to stay in this country. Get out of here before Tommy wakes up and he finds out I told you."

"Where in Tijuana?"

"I don't know. All I heard was Tijuana. I don't want Tommy to find out. Go."

I went into the hotel and left him to his dreams and illusions, his reputation still intact. He would probably tell Tommy that he had taken me and that I had run off. They would still have their five hundred dollars from Bobo and I had my information as to where Bobo was supposed to be holed up, without having to pay fifty dollars to get it. Bobo, in a sense, had actually paid to give away his own hiding place.

All in all, it wasn't such a bad deal, except my jaw was sore and swelling from where Tommy had landed that roundhouse right. Maybe Tommy really had been a contender.

Thirteen

Tijuana wasn't much in 1949—bars, whorehouses, American sailors and marines on the prowl, some tourists, and a growing reputation as a place to get about anything you had trouble getting on the San Diego side of the border. The permanent population lived in squalid shacks around the edges of the town that smelled of too many bars and too much raunchy nightlife. Wearing a blue sports coat, black trousers, and open-necked white shirt without tie, I joined the other Tijuana thrill seekers.

I didn't tell anybody why I was there. I thought that would be a good way of getting my head blown off by Bobo or somebody he hired to do it. Instead, I tried to blend in with the low nightlife, hoping to catch sight of Bobo or get a lead on where he was. I slowly drank Mexican beer and watched the strippers, occasionally having a hormonal interest in what I saw. Mostly, it was too gross to excite much interest in sex. But the drunken sailors and marines, who saw G-strings pulled down as crotches were thrown in their faces, thought it was great.

After about three hours of hanging out in the nightclubs and getting more of a buzz from the beer than I wanted to get, I saw Bobo come into a club with two girls. Bobo was wearing a black suit, white shirt and red tie. The girls were wearing tight black dresses and red high heels. He was laughing and seemed to be having a good time. The girls, only coming up to his chest, looked as if they were still in their teens or barely out of them. One of Bobo's big hands alternated in patting each of their butts as they went to a table and sat down on each side of him.

Bobo laid a wad of bills on the table and three more girls tried to join him. They were shooed away by Bobo's youthful beauties. Bobo frowned and then laughed. His two companions laughed uproariously.

I decided this was as good of a time as any to take him. I walked quickly over to his table, pulling my .38 out of its shoulder holster as I walked. I wanted the .38 prominently displayed to convince him to come peacefully with me. I stepped in front of the table.

"Party's over. Get up, Bobo, and let's take a walk."

He looked up and all the mirth in his face departed.

"Hello, private dick. I should have killed you."

"But you didn't. This isn't a social call. Let's get going or I'm going to have to bury you in lead."

He stood up, scowling. I motioned him to walk toward the door. Only a few people had noticed us. Most were watching the stripper who was gyrating on the runway that was lined with tables of heavily-drinking marines and sailors.

After we had taken a few steps across the open floor, someone from behind me grabbed my arm, pulling it downward. The hard pull on my arm caused me to pull the trigger, firing a bullet into the floor. This got everyone's attention, including my own.

I tried to shake off Bobo's two girls who were all over me like twin hellcats, kicking, biting, clawing, scratching. The .38 went flying.

"Leave him to me" Bobo called.

The girls were slow to get Bobo's message, but when they saw the look in his eyes, they got it. I got it too, and I knew his intent was to kill me with his bare hands.

Bobo slipped the right cross I leveled at his head. His powerful hands grabbed my shoulders and threw me into the table he and the girls had just vacated.

Coming up from the floor I smashed a wooden chair into his shoulder. He shrugged it off as if the chair had been no more than a fly. He swung a right hand that caught me on the chin and sent me sprawling.

A couple of bouncers came forward and started to grab Bobo. They were grabbed by marines and sailors who were yelling, "Let 'em fight!" The drunken marines and sailors were not to be denied a good spectacle.

As Bobo came toward me again, I yelled, "Semper Fi! An old marine buddy needs help!" I added my name, rank and serial number—"Martin Mayfield, Sergeant, 1503993, USMC!"—hoping it would help.

Loyalty in the Corps runs true and deep. A little guy jumped onto Bobo's back and then all hell broke lose. As marines plowed into Bobo, sailors plowed into them. Chairs went flying, heads were smashed, and blood started to run all over the place.

Bobo didn't stick around for the fight. He made for the door, tossing guys out of his way like a snowplow clearing a path.

After being hit on the side of the head by a sailor and then decking him with a left uppercut, I retrieved my .38 from the floor. As I picked it up I saw Bobo going through the swinging doors to the street.

I got through the swinging doors just in time to see Bobo

pull a taxi driver out of a yellow '48 Plymouth taxi. Bobo was driving away in the lumbering four-door sedan as I jumped on the rear bumper.

I tried to get a shot off through the back window, but Bobo turned a sharp corner and I went flying. As I rolled on the sidewalk I managed to protect my head and hold on to the .38 at the same time. I couldn't get a shot off at the fleeing yellow taxi because of the milling crowd that lined the street in search of nightlife.

I ran about a block to the '41 Merc and revved it up. The yellow Plymouth had a good lead, but I knew the Merc would catch it eventually. If I didn't get it, I figured the Border Patrol would stop it since Bobo was heading in the direction of San Diego.

Bobo didn't stop at the border-crossing station. He swung out around the line of five cars stopped at the border-crossing station and crashed through an unpainted wooden fence. The Plymouth must have been doing at least eighty when it plowed through it. I knew because the speedometer needle of the Merc was rocking around ninety. I drove the Merc through the same hole the taxi had opened in the fence.

The fence slowed the taxi enough for me to get two shots off at it by holding the .38 out the driver's side of the Merc. One of the shots hit the left rear tire and the Plymouth veered off the road. The Plymouth was built solid and it plowed through the wall and plateglass window that said "Jerry's Cafe." When it came to rest, a surprised waitress behind the counter and three sailors sitting at the counter watched Bobo crawl out of the smoking car and go out the hole the Plymouth had just bored in the cafe.

I would have preferred to take Bobo alive, but he left me no choice. From the side of the cafe he fired at me as I got out of the Merc. I fired twice, both shots hitting Bobo.

He was breathing and still conscious when I got up to him, sitting with his back against the wall where he had slid down. He was holding his stomach. His .38 lay in the dirt beside him.

I yelled at the waitress and the three sailors who had come

out the front of the cafe and were coming around the corner. "Call the cops and get an ambulance!"

Bobo was looking up at me with glazed eyes that showed his big body was in great pain.

"I didn't want to shoot you, Bobo. I wanted to take you alive."

He said nothing, and I didn't know if he heard me, but I wanted to get information out of him.

"Who hired you to kill Irene Berkowitz?"

"I didn't kill her," he said in a slow, measured tone, barely above a whisper. Leroy killed her. I wouldn't let him throw her over the side. She was beautiful. I propped her up by the side of the road so that she could look over the valley. She was beautiful."

"Where's Leroy? Was he your partner?"

"New York. We split. He went east. I went west. He's no good. He killed Irene. She was beautiful, but I wouldn't let him throw her over."

His voice was getting more halting. I still hadn't learned what I wanted to know, so I knew he had better tell me fast. I could see that his belly was drenched in blood.

"Who hired you and Leroy?"

His eyes were beginning to take on that distant look I had seen in the war, just before guys died. He didn't answer.

"Who hired you and Leroy?" I asked again, trying to break through the haze that was engulfing him.

"You shoot real good, private dick. You put me down for the long count. But you're O.K."

"Who hired you and Leroy?"

"Banker."

"A banker or was his name 'Banker'?"

"A banker."

"Give me a name, Bobo. What banker?"

"You figure it out, smart guy."

His lips bent into a weak smile and then he was gone. He looked peaceful as I closed his eyelids. The pain was gone from his face.

"You're O.K. too, Bobo," I said half to myself. "You shouldn't have hung around with bums."

Fourteen

Crashing through the fence at the border and pumping two slugs into Bobo made national news. Instead of curbing my fame, I had fed it. So much for being an ordinary guy and wanting to do an ordinary job.

I left California fast enough to avoid questions by the press, but when I got back to Denver, reporters and photographers were camped at both the Pig and Poke and at Galliger's car lot. As I was to learn later, Joe loved the publicity, thinking it might sell cars. Frank, on the other hand, was tired of reporters and photographers occupying booths for hours on a nickel cup of coffee. Instead of the publicity bringing him business, members of the press took space that normally went to legitimate customers.

It was at the Pig and Poke in the late afternoon that I faced the reporters and photographers. I had just gotten in from the road and I looked as bad as the Merc. It had dust and dirt all over it and so did I. It had some scratches from where it had followed the taxi through the fence at the border. I had bumps and bruises from the fight in the nightclub and from where I had bounced on the sidewalk when the taxi threw me. I had left California so fast that I hadn't had time to change my clothes or have the car's oil changed. The Merc needed a grease job, oil change, and wash. I needed a shave, shower, and a bourbon and water.

I tried to slip around the restaurant to the motel courtyard in back where my room, number three, was located, but one of the reporters saw me and they all vacated the restaurant.

"Hey, Mayfield, we've been waiting for you," somebody yelled.

"'Give me a break, will you? As you can see, I just got in and I'm not looking my best."

Flash bulbs began to pop and a woman reporter in a blue suit yelled, "Tell us about it, Mr. Mayfield. How did you catch him?"

So much for the press giving a guy a break.

"Catch who?" I asked, knowing who she meant, but deciding I wouldn't make it easy for them.

"Bernard Taskovitch," Jeffrey Morgan from the Denver Post called out. I had seen him around enough to know him. He had an English accent and he covered the crime beat. He had silver-gray hair and a matching neatly-clipped mustache. His kind face looked as though he over-indulged in gin and tonic.

"That was his name? Jeffrey, you've got to be kidding."

They laughed.

"Now you see why he went by Bobo," Jeffrey replied. They laughed again.

"Well, Bernard Taskovitch or Bobo, the Heart," I said, deciding Bobo deserved more dignity than a laugh, "he was one hell of a guy. He was tough, but he had a heart, and I want you guys to print that. When he was dying, he told me he didn't kill Irene Berkowitz; his partner did. I doubt that Bobo ever killed anybody, but I don't know that for a fact. He was a victim of bad company. You guys ought to be careful when you hang around with each other."

They laughed and then somebody asked, "If he was such a good guy, how come you had to plug him?"

"When somebody is throwing hot lead at you, you don't have much choice. I would have preferred to take him alive."

"Where is his partner and are you going after him, Mr. Mayfield?" the woman in the blue suit asked, looking up from her note pad. She looked about thirty, had black hair and high cheek bones. She was very attractive. I hadn't seen her around before. Her eyes appeared to be soft-brown from where I was standing.

"You guys can learn from her. Hear that? She called me Mr. Mayfield."

They laughed for a second before someone said, "O.K., Mayfield, do you know where he is and are you going after him?"

"That type of thing is better left to the police," I said while yawning and stroking my nearly three-day growth of beard. "I'm not going anywhere except to a shave, a shower, and to bed when you guys let me off the hook. At this point, I'm not even sure I know where my room is, much less where Bobo's partner is."

"Are you terribly tired, Mr. Mayfield?"

"Now, there's a lady with manners," I said, pointing to the woman in the blue suit. "What paper do you work for, sweetheart? I'll tell you anything you want to know after I've had a good night's sleep. These other inconsiderate bums may never find out the true story."

I said it in such a way that the reporters knew I wasn't really calling them bums, but that I was tired. I was careful with the press because I knew they could help or hinder me in my work.

"I work for the *Rocky Mountain News* and I'll hold you to an exclusive interview."

The other reporters hooted and howled. The *Rocky Mountain News* reporter looked embarrassed. "I didn't mean it that way," she said. "I just want a story like you do."

They hooted again until somebody called, "Give us the details, Mayfield. How did you find Bobo and how did you take him?"

"What paper do you work for, pal?" I said, drawing attention away from the *Rocky Mountain News* reporter. She looked at me in an appreciative way as if she understood what I was doing. She was close enough now that I could see the beauty of her round, brown eyes.

"*Kansas City Star*."

"That far away," I said.

"You're big news, Mayfield. So, how about some details of what went on?"

I let the press work me over for another fifteen minutes or so and then I called a halt, feigning complete exhaustion. "You guys know where I live," I said, "but how about keeping it out of the papers? I don't mind talking to you on occasion, but I would prefer not to have to be asked a lot of questions by curious sightseers. Anything they want to know, they can read in the papers." I was close to falling down, but not quite. I could still function as I unlocked the door to number three.

They must have liked what I said, because none of the local papers mentioned my address. I don't know what the out-of-town papers said, but who would want to drive to Denver to see an ordinary private detective anyway?

The stories in the *Rocky Mountain News* and the *Denver Post* were flattering to me. They told of a local, tough-guy detective erasing a good guy who went wrong in bad company. The reporting was good, but most of all, I liked the human interest angle the *Rocky Mountain News* did in a separate story. It was written by Delana Dixon, who I guessed was the woman in the blue suit. She told of my exhaustion and my politeness to the reporters. She told of the compassion I had for the man I had killed. She even used the words "ruggedly handsome" when referring to me.

The lady in the blue suit would get her exclusive interview if she wanted it. My mind also began toying with how she might be useful to me in finding who the banker was that Bobo had referred to before he died.

Fifteen

Audrey Berkowitz called the next day and left word with Joe Galliger for me to come to her apartment in Golden, which I did. Since the burning of her family home, she had taken a small apartment—living room, bedroom, half-kitchen, and bath. It was nice, but not luxurious.

Audrey's concern for me seemed genuine, but Barry Hampton was there, so I couldn't fully gauge what romantic feelings she had toward me, if any. We had gotten pretty chummy on the train, but you never really know about a thing like that. I had just rescued her from kidnappers, so maybe she was just being grateful.

Barry Hampton said he was grateful for my elimination of Bobo. He said it made him feel safer about Audrey, since one of the thugs was no longer in action. He asked if I would be going after the other one.

"Where do I look? He could be in Canada, for all I know," I said noncommittally.

"Have you got any leads on him?"

As Hampton asked the question, he sounded a little more urgent than I expected him to be. Maybe it was just his interest in the case; then again, maybe he knew something he wasn't telling me or he had something to hide, I continued my noncommittal answers.

"Bobo told me the other guy killed Irene. That's about it.'"

"You could just let the police handle it. You did more than enough by just protecting Audrey. As far as I'm concerned, this case was closed when you wiped out the kidnappers on the train. You earned that five thousand dollars I gave you."

Audrey looked at me appreciatively. "Yes, Marty, you certainly have done an outstanding job. I would give you a grade of 'A.'"

"Which reminds me, Mayfield, here's a little something for getting rid of Bobo."

Hampton handed me a check and I glanced at it. It was for another thousand dollars. I stuffed it into my brown sports coat pocket and mumbled my thanks.

"Now, if you should decide to go after the other one, I want to know about it. Should you need more money, I can supply it. If you keep me informed, I can sweeten the pot for you. You've earned every dollar I've paid you. I'm willing to pay more. On the other hand, if you have no leads on the other guy and you want to drop the case now, that's pretty understandable."

Hampton seemed a little too-encouraging for me to get off the case. He was willing to pay for me getting the other guy, but he wanted to be "informed." Maybe it was just a normal reaction from a guy who was kicking out a lot of dough.

"The money is appreciated, but isn't it getting a little expensive for you?"

Audrey laughed and said, "Barry can afford it." Seeing the

frown Hampton gave her, she added, "He's a private detective. If he doesn't already know your family is quite wealthy, he could find it out easily enough."

"And just what business is your family in, Hampton?"

"Mostly banking," he replied.

My brain said, "bingo" but my lips said, "I guess that explains it. Banks have money. You're in banking, so you've got money. I assumed when you took me to 'your bank' to get some money for me, it wasn't really 'your bank,' but just a bank where you had an account. Boy, do I feel dumb. I didn't know you owned the place. Now, about another ten grand or so; anytime you want to drop a little more on me, feel free to do so."

They saw the humor in the remark and smiled.

"No, I think you've got about all you need for now. Besides, my family isn't really as wealthy as Audrey implies. But, if you decide to go after the other guy and want to be reimbursed for your trouble, let me know."

When I left Audrey and Hampton, it was about three in the afternoon. It was a little early for drinking at the Red Horse, but it was a place where reporters and the general public didn't know I would be. The eight-foot-long red stallion statue, in a full run above the door, with legs stretched out and tail flying, made the place easy to identify. The bar stood in an open field at the edge of town near the intersection of Alameda Avenue and Sheridan Boulevard, with no other businesses around.

Red, the owner, seemed to be hung up on the color red. He went by the name Red. He had the red stallion above the entrance. The building was painted red. There were red letters on the five-foot-square white sign on the side of the building. The letters said RED HORSE BAR AND GRILL. Inside, it was just a normal bar and grill, without the color red splashed over anything except the red-cushioned bar stools and the red cushions on the booth benches. For this, I was grateful, because, by the time you got into the place, you didn't want to see much more of the color red.

"It's a little early in the day for you, isn't it?" Beverly

asked from behind the bar as I took a stool at the opposite end
from where two guys were drinking draws. I thought of her as
"Bountiful Beverly." She was a little on the heavy side, over
forty in both age and bra size, rough on the edges, but still very
pleasant to look at. On occasion, she had helped Red throw out
a rowdy customer. She was all woman and then some, with a
round face, a curl of a double chin, brown eyes and dyed
blonde hair, short flat nose and sensuous mouth. She usually
wore a sweater and slacks, as she was doing today.

"Yeah, I know, but I needed a quiet place to think."

"Well, Marty, we got lots of quiet today. As you can see,
we aren't busting at the seams with business."

"You got a cook on?"

"No, but Red will cook you something. He's in the back
doing book work, but he'll cook whatever you want, if he's got
it."

"Tell him to give me some steak and eggs. I've been
hungry ever since I got back from California. I could stand a
second breakfast."

"With you splashed all over the papers, I can see why you
might need a little quiet. If you did what they said you did, I
can see why you might be eating a little more than usual. How
big of a steak you want and how many eggs?"

"Big steak and four eggs."

"You sure you had a breakfast already today?"

"I ate at the Pig and Poke about noon. Give me my eggs
over hard and the steak well-done. I'll take a bourbon and
water while I'm waiting. I'll have coffee with the steak and
eggs."

"You got it."

When she set the bourbon and water on the counter in front
of me, I picked up the drink and moved over to a booth,
lighting up a Lucky in the process. I began to mull over the
meeting that morning with Audrey and Barry Hampton.

Hampton seemed to be throwing money at me every
chance he got. A grateful client or somebody who didn't want
me to look too critically at him? Bobo mentioned a banker

hiring him. Hampton's family was in the banking business. Maybe it was just a coincidence. Originally, I had bought the story about him wanting to protect Audrey from whoever had killed her sister and father. I suppose I still believed him, but I was beginning to have some doubts.

My thoughts were interrupted by Red setting the plate of steak and eggs down in front of me. He was wearing a white T-shirt and white cook's hat and white cook's apron. His fat belly bulged the apron. His bald head didn't show under the cook's hat. His once-red eyebrows had turned gray. He still had a mass of red freckles, which indicated why he had been given the name Red.

"What's wrong with Beverly, Red? You just let her carry drinks?" Beverly was down at the end of the bar, talking to the two guys who were drinking beer.

"I just wanted to welcome you back from your California trip. Anything wrong with that?"

"I'm flattered. How's business, Red?"

"At night, the joint jumps. From noon to one, pretty good. The afternoon stinks but I open at noon so I'll get the lunchtime crowd. So, how's it with you, Marty? The papers pretty accurate?"

"They're pretty accurate, Red, except they don't tell you how hungry I have been since getting back from California. Yesterday, I ate like a horse. Today, I'm still hungry as hell."

"Well, dig in, Marty. It must be nice to be your age and eat like that. I remember it. You want more, I'll cook it."

"Thanks, Red."

I watched Red amble off. At sixty-three years old, he was having a problem with arthritis. It didn't seem to bother him all the time. Today, it was bothering him.

After finishing the steak and eggs and a cup of black coffee, I made two quick telephone calls. One was to Harry Makris at the D.P.D. The other was to Delana Dixon at the *Rocky Mountain News*. I asked them both to come to the Red Horse. I gave Harry no special instruction, knowing he would keep it quiet. For Delana, I added a few words of instruction.

"Miss Dixon, this is Martin Mayfield. Is it Miss or Mrs.?"

"It was Mrs. It's now Miss. How nice to hear from you, Mr. Mayfield."

"Would you be willing to meet me at the Red Horse Bar and Grill, Miss Dixon?"

She didn't hesitate before answering, "Yes. Where is it?"

"You've never heard of the Red Horse, Denver's most famous bar and grill?" I said jokingly.

"I'm afraid not."

"Alameda and Sheridan. The west side of town, the south side of Alameda. And, Miss Dixon, would you not tell anyone about our meeting. You know how nosy reporters can be. "

She laughed. "Yes, I know. What time, and will I have trouble locating it?"

"As soon as it's convenient for you. I don't think you'll have any trouble identifying it."

"I'm on my way," she said and hung up.

I had another cup of coffee while waiting for her and Harry. I decided I would have the next bourbon and water when they got there.

Sixteen

Delana Dixon got there first. I was glad because it gave us about fifteen minutes to be alone before Harry arrived, if you can call it being alone as the Red Horse began to pick up additional patrons—construction workers and salesman types—who were just getting off work.

I stood as she seated herself across from me in the booth. "Peach is a nice color for you," I said as I sat back down. "Do you always wear suits?"

"Suits are my working wardrobe. Since it's a warm summer day, I happen to be in peach. Don't you like ties?"

"I'm not fond of wearing them. I wear them when I think my professional appearance requires it. Most of the time, I like to just wear a sports coat and a white shirt with the top button

unbuttoned, as I'm doing today with this brown sports coat.
It's a lot more comfortable. Ties are only good in the winter-
time when it's cold. I imagine they started out as scarves to
protect against the cold and then they became ties. They were
for warmth, not adornment. They have become the most
useless part of a man's clothing, purely decorative in warm
weather. Today is warm, so I'm not being decorated."

"And I suppose you don't like decorative things, Mr.
Mayfield?"

"I didn't say that. You look pretty decorative and I like
you. And please call me Marty. After all, you are sitting in a
bar with me, so I suppose we can be on a first-name basis."

"Well, Marty, do you think I'm functional as well as
decorative?"

"We will just have to wait and see, won't we? Beautiful
things can also be functional."

She kind of bowed her head in a feigned blush like Bette
Davis might do in the movies. Come to think of it, she did
remind me of Bette Davis, except her eyes were round brown
instead of Bette Davis' soft blue.

"Marty it is, and I'm Delana." When she pronounced her
name, the "a's" had an "ah" sound like in "Lana." She
extended a hand across the booth and I gently shook it by
holding her fingers. "Now, Marty, what did you want to see
me about? Is it time for my exclusive interview?"

"Not so fast. I know your name, that you write for the
Rocky, that you wear suits and that you're very attractive, in
a decorative, perhaps functional, way. Shouldn't I know a few
more things before we get down to business?"

"There's not much more. I grew up in San Francisco;
studied journalism at Stanford; graduated in 1942; went to
work for a government agency in Washington during the
remainder of the war; married an Army captain who was on
General Marshall's staff in Washington. After the war, he
returned to his family farm near Grand Junction, Colorado.
They grow peaches and other things. I was bored stiff working
on a small-town newspaper and the marriage just didn't work

out for us. We divorced and I got a job with the *Rocky Mountain News*. California to Washington, to Grand Junction, to Denver—there, you've got it all. No children, no husband, and no desire to have either. Just a happy career woman."

"You are functional as well as decorative. Any bitterness over the marriage and divorce?" I asked, knowing I was getting a little more personal than I should have been.

"None. He is a nice guy. We were just two different people. I like the city. He likes the country. I want a career. He wants children. What else is there to say?" She looked sharply at me, as if expecting a reproof. Seeing and hearing none, she said, "Now, it's your turn. One good life story deserves another."

"Mine is not nearly so glamorous. I grew up in Denver and graduated from high school. I spent a few years at the tail end of the Depression riding freights and looking for work. During those years, among other things, I worked as a lumberjack, highway construction worker, and section hand on the railroad. I even shipped out of your hometown on a freighter for six months. I was going nowhere except from job to job, so I enrolled at the University of Colorado to study I didn't know what. Tojo interrupted my education plans and I went off to the Pacific with the Marine Corps. I was an enlisted man, so I'll have to forgive you for marrying a captain. Officers always seem to collect the glory but not the sweat. I came back from the war, after being laid up in the hospital for awhile, and then went to Denver University on the G.I. Bill to study I didn't know what some more. The second semester I took a class in criminology. That was it; I had found something that suited my independent and sometimes obnoxious ways. I dropped out of school and became a private detective. I've been very happy ever since. I have no wives, no children, and only those responsibilities I wish to assume. I like it that way."

"If you grew up in Denver, you must have family and a lot of friends here."

"No family and very few friends. The family has been

dead for years. They were mostly drunks. I'm not in the business of making friends. I have many acquaintances, but only a few friends. The less you expect of people, the less they will disappoint you."

I could see she wanted to ask more, but she didn't, which was good, because that is all I would have told her anyway.

"Now that we know each other," I said, "let's get down to business. Ever worked in a bank?"

"No."

"Would you like to work in one?"

"Not especially. I'm a reporter and I like it just fine."

"But reporters like to get the big story," I said, holding the carrot in front of her.

"Just what big story is that?"'

"Delana," I continued, "from here on, what I say goes only to you and Harry, who should be showing up soon."

"Who is Harry?"

"A police detective friend of mine. You will meet him when he gets here. What I'm telling you is strictly confidential."

"Tell a reporter something and expect it to be confidential; you've got to be kidding."

"No, I'm not, and I know I can trust you." I didn't know that, but I hoped it might be true.

"You're right, Marty; you can trust me." There was a look in her eyes, that had I been tuned into it better, could have generated sexual tension between us. It was a look of "I really do want to help you and I would be willing to give you anything you asked for, including myself." I don't think I was reading more into the look than was really there, but I skipped the look, thinking we could work on romance at some future date when we really did know each other better.

"I have reason to believe that the two foreign agents were not behind the killing of Irene Berkowitz and her father. Just before Bobo took the deep six, he told me that a banker had hired him and his partner to kill Irene. That's where you come in."

I didn't get to explain right away because Harry Makris

interrupted with his arrival. He was sore at me for not telling him I was going to California after Bobo. He wanted to be informed, just as Barry Hampton wanted to be informed. This time, I would tell Harry that I was going to New York after Leroy. I would still leave Hampton uninformed. Hampton had become my leading suspect in the killing-for-hire of Irene Berkowitz and her father Professor Berkowitz. Maybe I could sweat the truth out of Leroy before somebody else or I killed him. In the meantime, Delana and Harry could work on the bank angle, if Delana and her boss at the newspaper would go along with what I had in mind.

After introducing Harry, pacifying him with a bottle of Coors, and letting him know I wanted to inform him of what was happening next, I was ready to explain my plan. Harry was seated next to me, enjoying the view of Delana. He was sipping at his beer, never drinking more than one at any sitting. I was drinking a bourbon and water, refraining from smoking because I knew Harry didn't like sitting next to a smoker. Delana was drinking a dry martini; she was as slow a drinker as Harry.

"Now, Harry, since we've all been formally introduced, perhaps I can go on telling Delana why I want her to go to work in the same bank where Irene Berkowitz worked before she was killed."

"I haven't agreed to anything yet," Delana said to Harry. "Your friend seems to have some wild idea about me getting a big story for my paper."

"He is full of surprises and other things," Harry said in a way that I could tell he was still a little sore at me.

"Mind your manners, Harry, and perhaps you can get who hired the thugs to kill Irene. Delana can get her big story, and I'll go fetch Bobo's partner."

"I thought the foreign agents hired the thugs to kill Irene. As for Bobo's partner, what makes you think you can find him when we can't?"

"I won't answer that. But as to the foreign agents, Bobo told me it was a banker who had hired the killing."

"Why didn't you tell me that when you first got back?"

"Because I haven't seen you until now, and I wanted to think about how we could best use that information. Putting the whole police department out to look for a banker probably wouldn't net us anything. If Bobo was telling the truth, perhaps we can locate our banker by putting a plant in the bank where Irene worked. That would be Delana here, with the permission of her boss, who is the only one on the paper who is to know. You, Harry, are to be her police contact and protection. I'll see what I can come up with by trying to bring back Bobo's partner from New York?"

"How do you know he is in New York?" Harry asked, obviously surprised.

"Bobo told me before he died."

"Sounds like he spilled his guts to you."

"In more ways that one. But the important thing is that we've got a line on who else might be involved. I think it is worth a week or two of your time, Delana, to bring in a big story for your paper. What do you say?"

"I'll talk to my boss Paul Horn. He likes crazy schemes. He might like this. What makes you think I can get a job at the bank?"

"I'll leave that to you—intelligent, resourceful, beautiful, but don't take any chances that might endanger your life. That's what you got Harry here for. He's one of the few people I might trust with my life, and I mean that."

Harry looked flattered. "What do you think she ought to look for? Anything else you've been holding out on me? Besides, what makes you think we've got the right bank?"

"Barry Hampton's family is in the banking business. I checked, and the bank where Irene worked was controlled by the Hampton family."

"I thought we decided Hampton was clean."

"We did, but if Bobo was telling the truth, there is a good chance Hampton's dirty. Irene worked at a bank controlled by the Hamptons. Irene is killed by thugs who were hired by a banker. It is possible that Barry Hampton or someone in his family or bank is behind the killings."

"It doesn't add up," Harry said, starting his annoying habit of stroking his mustache. "Why were the thugs working for foreign agents? How could they be working for foreign agents and a banker? I guess it could be both rather than either. If the banker was trying to kill the family and the foreign agents were trying to kidnap the family, how come they were using the same set of thugs?"

"I don't know, Harry, but maybe if I get Bobo's partner and you and Delana work on the banking angle, we might get lucky and put this all together."

"What makes you think you can find Bobo's partner in New York? New York City, New York State, it's a big place with a lot of people."

"Thanks for the geography lesson, Harry. I admit it might be tough, but I may get some help. Delana, would you powder your nose or something? I want to tell Harry a couple of things that I don't want you to know. I trust you, but there is no need to let information get around that could get a guy killed. I have sources that Harry needs to know, but you don't need to know."

Delana looked at me with less-than-friendly eyes. "You want me planted in a bank where I might run into a killer and you don't want me to know all about the case."

"This has nothing to do with anything you need to know about the case. When people help me, I don't violate their confidence. With Harry, it will go no further. With you being a reporter and all, it might slip out sometime when you're not even thinking. Please, Delana, let me just tell Harry how I nailed Bobo and how I might nail his partner."

The word "please" sometimes does wonders. It can be a powerful word and that is why I don't use it very often. Delana didn't seemed miffed anymore.

"Want me to stick around for anything after you have told him?" she said in a pleasanter tone than I expected.

"Yes. You and Harry need to talk a little about your banking business. While you are doing that, I'll go put on a tie and come back to take you someplace nice for dinner—that is, if you would consider going out with me."

She hesitated a moment, I think more to tease me than anything else. "Invitation accepted. I'll sit at that empty booth over there while you talk to Harry. If one of those guys at the bar tries to pick me up, I hope you will rescue me."

"If he doesn't, I will," Harry said.

"Please, Harry, you are a married man," I said.

"Oh, you know what I mean," Harry grumbled.

Delana sat in the booth for about five minutes while I told Harry how Frank Brodrick had supplied the tip that had led to Bobo. I told him Frank had suggested that if I wanted to find Leroy in New York that I hang out in Jack Dempsey's restaurant. Frank had said that he would send word to one of his contacts in New York that I wanted Leroy. Frank had liked the nice things I had told the paper about Bobo. He thought Leroy was a rat who had aided Bobo on his way to ruin, so he was going to help me get him.

My keeping-Harry-informed concluded, I went to rescue Delana from the guys who swarmed about her. It hadn't taken long for her good looks to draw the guys off their bar stools. I left her in the protection of Harry while I went home to change into a black suit and tie and to throw on a little after-shave lotion. I had decided Delana was worth the tie, the suit, the skin bracer, and the price of two dinners and drinks at one of Denver's finest.

The evening verged on high-class pleasant. I wasn't usually high class, but I could pretend at times. I took her to Tyler's Supper Club out on West Colfax between Denver and Golden. They had a stage show, an orchestra, and dancing. After we had dined and listened to the comedian, I held her in my arms while swaying to the music. She was as feminine and sexually appealing as any woman I had ever held.

I didn't try to take her to my motel room, because I didn't want to spoil what we had going. I wanted the first time, if there was to be a first time, to be just right, maybe flowers, champagne, soft music, and silk sheets. I could take my chances on waiting. Some things are worth the wait. If you wait and they never happen, what could have been is sometimes as sweet in your memory as what did happen. When it comes down to it, memory and what happens are all the same, a fleeting glimpse of time that gives us pleasure or pain. Delana Dixon was giving me pleasure that was worth sipping slowly.

Seventeen

Jack Dempsey had traded on his name as a former heavy-weight champion to go into the restaurant business. When I got off the airplane in New York, I did two things: I checked into a hotel and started hanging out at Jack Dempsey's restaurant.

With the use of the Dempsey name and affable greeting of the customers by Dempsey when he was in town, the restaurant was one of the most popular in New York City. Sportsmen, journalists, celebrities, the wealthy, and some ordinary stiffs like myself attended. Jack Dempsey, now in his fifties, was a gracious host, shaking hands and signing autographs. The former champ still looked rugged as hell, but he seemed to have a heart of gold.

I thought of telling Dempsey I was from Colorado when I shook his hand, knowing that was where he had been born and got his start fighting, but I decided he had enough people jawing at him without me celebrity-clawing too. I didn't know if he knew why I was hanging around the place or even if I stood out from the crowd enough to be noticed. I had made up my mind to wait a full week before I went hunting for Leroy on my own. The bartender knew my name, so I figured that if anybody wanted to see me, all they had to do was ask. On the third day of waiting, somebody did ask at about two in the afternoon. The guy was young, maybe in his mid-twenties.

"You Martin Mayfield?" The voice was soft and calm. The face was almost a baby face, with light complexion and blondish hair and eyebrows. The body wore a loud yellow tie, blue-and-yellow-checked sports coat, blue shirt, black trousers and black porkpie hat. The eyes were clear blue with an expression of ice in them. I doubted that this guy was your typical social worker.

"Yes."

"Follow me."

I got up from my seat at the bar, leaving the last part of the draw that I had been sipping. I disliked beer, but you could drag out three or four beers all day if you were careful and added some pretzels to the mix. Drinking bourbon and water all day could get you plastered and where would a guy in my business be if his brain was floating in booze?

As I followed him out into the bright sunshine, I noted that he was about my height. His shoulders were back and he had a cocky walk. I decided he was a little too brash for his own good, which meant he was either dumb or felt completely safe in his abilities or his position. I thought it was the latter because he didn't strike me as dumb.

When we arrived at a shiny black '48 Cadillac four-door sedan with white sidewalls, he opened the back door, stood aside and said, "Get in."

I looked at the driver and the guy sitting beside him. They were less flamboyant than the guy who had led me out of the bar, but the car and their dress also added up to "mob."

"Why should I?"

"You want Leroy. We might give him to you, if you check out."

"Good enough," I said and slid into the back seat. Ice eyes followed me in. The Cadillac pulled away from the curb with a quiet rumble of its motor.

Cadillac, with this model, had made the back of the car as interesting as the front by adding a slight lift to the back fenders. They were being called tailfins and I liked the design change.

"This is a '48 isn't it? How come you boys are a year behind?" I wanted them to talk so that I could tell what they knew and how hostile they were toward me. If they seemed less-than-friendly, it might be a setup. Instead of taking me to Leroy, I might be heading for a permanent bath in the East River.

"You ever ride in a Cadillac before?"' ice eyes asked. The accent was decidedly New York City, probably Brooklyn.

"Oh, once or twice."

"The boss says you're from Denver. To me, that's hicksville. How would a guy from hicksville get to ride in a Cadillac?" Ice eyes showed no emotion, but the two guys in the front seat snickered.

"We've got a car or two in Denver, but mostly we just ride around on horses, looking for guys from New York to beat the hell out of."

Ice eyes brought his hand up from the right pocket of his sports jacket. It held a .38-caliber revolver. I knew he had been holding it since he first approached me in the restaurant. The guy in the front passenger seat scowled at me over his shoulder.

"Why don't I just shoot you, loud mouth?" ice eyes said.

"You could, but if you've got a boss, he told you not to shoot me. At least, not here; otherwise, you would have done it already. So, what are we doing? Are you guys taking me to see your boss or taking me for a ride? If it's to see your boss, there's no need to quarrel. Since your buddy is sitting in the front seat rather than back here with us, I figure this is just a friendly ride. Otherwise, you would have me squeezed in the back seat and both of you would be holding rods on me."

"Pretty smart, hicksville." Ice eyes put the pistol back in his pocket but continued to hold it. "You know, you shouldn't say bad things about guys from New York. We were rubbing guys out when you guys in the West were still sucking cow tits."

The guys in the front seat laughed.

"Don't knock it unless you've tried it. It beats jacking off with stray dogs like you guys in New York do."

The guys in the front seat hesitated and then guffawed again. Ice eyes couldn't make up his mind how to react. Finally, he decided to say nothing and I did likewise.

We pulled up at a neighborhood liquor store. When three of us got out of the car, I followed ice eyes into the liquor store, with the guy who hadn't been driving, following me. We went by a couple of clerks, who looked more like "mob" than clerks, and then we went up the stairs in the back of the liquor store.

Five guys were playing poker in a smoky room over the liquor store. Fans were blowing off to the side to circulate the air but not the money. It was not penny ante because big bills were all over the table and the pot was full of fifties and hundreds.

They stopped playing and looked up when the three of us entered. A heavy-set guy with dark wavy hair, pudgy fingers, and a fat unlit cigar he was chewing, spoke. He looked directly at me.

"Mayfield, why do you want Leroy?"

"He killed a girl and her father."

"Was he working with Communist agents?"

"I don't know all the details,'" I said, "but there were three foreign agents involved in kidnapping an American girl. Leroy was working for the foreign agents at that time. I was hired to protect her and I got her back. I figure the case isn't over until I get Leroy and anybody else who was involved with the killings and kidnapping."

"Yeah, we know. We read about you in the papers. We don't like any of our boys working for Communist agents. We figure Leroy shouldn't have tried to freelance on us." He paused and looked at the guys around the table. "See what happens when you freelance, and if any of you have any ideas 'bout working for the Communists or freelancing, you can forget it. This country has been good to us and we're not going to do anything to help turn it over to the Communists." He looked at me. "You can have him, Mayfield, but you got to take him our way."

"Thanks," I said. The attention shifted from me back to the poker game as if I weren't there. Ice eyes motioned me with his head to leave.

They dropped me back at Jack Dempsey's restaurant. As I got out of the car I said, "I thought you were taking me to see our mutual acquaintance."

"Tonight," ice eyes said from inside the back of the car. "You packing a rod, Mayfield?"

"I never go anyplace without it."

"Bring it. We'll pick you up here at 10 P.M. We'll have him where you can take him."

As I watched the Cadillac roll away, I wondered what they had in mind. The guy with the cigar had said I could have Leroy, but I would have to take him their way. I wasn't very keen about doing things the mob's way. I wished it were Denver instead of New York City and I had Harry Makris to rely on as back-up. New York suddenly seemed very cold in July.

Eighteen

They picked me up in the same Cadillac they were driving earlier in the day. It was a warm night; New York City didn't seem to cool off at night like Denver. As I got into the back of the Cadillac next to ice eyes, he asked, "How come you're not wearing a tie?"

"Maybe, being from Denver, I'm just a little too uncivilized to wear one all the time. I did put on my best brown sports coat and a clean white shirt."

"We like to look professional when we do a job," ice eyes said with obvious disappointment at my dress.

"Consider it a learning experience, working with a guy from Denver. Everybody doesn't do things the way they do them in New York City."

"I don't think I like you."

"I'm not overly fond of you either. So, where's Leroy? Let's get this over so we don't have to enjoy each other's company more than we have to."

"You'll know where he's at when I think you should know," ice eyes said petulantly.

"Why don't you quit fingering that gun in your pocket?" I said with a show of my own petulance. "It might go off and shoot your balls off."

The two guys in the front tried not to laugh, but they did.

"Shut up! You lugs want me to plant a bullet in him and you?"

"Take it easy," the guy on the passenger side of the front seat said while looking over his shoulder. "Some of the stuff he says is kind of funny."

"Thanks, pal. I'm glad the people in New York have a sense of humor. Your buddy here seems to be overly serious. If we work together in Denver sometime, you can laugh all you want."

"We got serious work to do," ice eyes said. "A professional takes his job serious."

I thought of saying something cute, but decided not to. I didn't want to antagonize ice eyes more than I already had. I said, "Yeah, I guess you're right."

"That's better," ice eyes said, thinking he had won a great moral victory. We rode the rest of the way in silence.

The driver remained in the car with the motor running while the three of us got out of the car. Ice eyes still held his pistol in his pocket. The other guy put his hand where I thought his shoulder holster was and started looking up and down the street. The street was deserted except for several kids playing kick the can under a streetlight at the end of the block. I guessed they were out past their bedtime because a woman was calling them and motioning them to come in.

"We made it easy for you." Ice eyes handed me a key. "He's in room 404. He'll be with a woman. She's one of ours. She knows you are coming. She'll have him in the bedroom with the lights on. She'll take a powder as soon as you come in. Kill him."

"Why can't I just make a pinch and take him to the cops?"

"And let him spill what he knows about us? The boss says to take care of him. You take care of him or we take care of him and you.'"

I started to walk toward the tenement.

"Wait a minute. I'm not through giving instructions yet." Ice eyes reached into his pocket and pulled out a switchblade knife. He pressed the button and watched the blade fly open.

He seemed to be enjoying this part of his instruction and wanted to prolong lt. He turned the blade back and forth in the dim light with his wrist.

"What's that for?"

"Cut off his ear and bring it to me." For the first time, he smiled. "That's how we got proof you did the job." He laughed.

I took the knife by the open blade and closed it, putting it into my brown sports coat pocket.

"Don't try anything different from the way I just told you. You do it different or try to run out on us and you're dead. We got people on the payroll all over New York, coppers too. You will never leave the city alive. Make sure you get him good. We don't like no sloppy work. Here in New York we're professionals."

"Yeah, I can see that," I said as I started for the front of the rooming house.

My brain was turning the situation over as I walked. When I killed him, I figured they would kill me. They didn't want me squawking to the cops about their part in killing Leroy anymore than they wanted Leroy squawking to the cops about their gang-land activities. This way, they would be getting rid of two sources of friction: one of their own who had freelanced and a nosy out-of-town private dick who was sniffing too close to gang-land activity. I had to think fast if I wanted information about the banker out of Leroy and wanted to save my life.

By the time I walked up the stairs to the fourth floor, I had no ideas. I decided I would just have to play it as it happened. If either Leroy or I, or both of us, ended up dead, then that was the way it had to be. It was my intention to make it turn out differently.

The key opened the door without any difficulty. I drew my .38 as I went toward the shaft of light coming out of the partially open bedroom door. I raised my left foot and pushed the door open with my shoe.

Leroy was lying flat on his back on the bed, naked except for yellow and black argyle socks. The bed was an iron four-poster, painted white. Leroy's wrists and ankles were tied to the four corners with brown leather straps. His mouth was gagged with a black scarf. His body was in a state of sexual arousal that quickly passed as his frightened eyes looked at me and the .38. The woman, naked and not too bad for her age, picked up her clothes and fled into the next room. I could hear her putting her clothes on as I tried to decide what to do with Leroy.

"You remember me, Leroy. You don't have much time if you want to live. When I take this gag off, you had better start talking, and I mean fast. You don't sing and I splatter your brains all over this four-poster."

My left hand pulled the knife from my pocket and switched it open to create an even more menacing appearance. With my right hand holding the .38, I used the knife in the left hand to slip under the gag on Leroy's cheekbone and cut upward. The gag fell away. "If you don't spill your guts fast enough, I may cut off that thing you were having so much fun with. Who hired you to kill Irene Berkowitz?"

His eyes were rolling around in his head and he was sweating. "Those guys you killed on the train."

I touched the tip of the knife blade to his windpipe. "One more lie and you're gone."

"It was a banker or something," he sputtered.

"What was his name?"

"I don't know. He wouldn't tell us. He gave us ten Gs, five for the daughter and five for the old man."

"How did you get to working for those foreigners?"

"The banker had us shadowing the sister until he decided whether or not he wanted us to knock her off too. The foreigners spotted us and offered us fifteen Gs to go to work for them. We did and all we had to do was be a little muscle for their security; that is, until they brought you in and wanted us to knock you off. We made another five Gs out of you. Those foreigners were rolling in dough. Then we took it on the lamb."

I cut the leather straps with the knife, knowing I was pressing my luck with the torpedoes outside by taking so much time with Leroy. "Get you clothes on," I growled as I closed the switchblade and put it back into my pocket.

As Leroy dressed, my eyes wandered around the room. I saw what I was looking for.

"Hurry it up!" I snapped in an attempt to get Leroy to go even faster than he was already going. I think it was a combination of fear and nakedness that made him move so fast into his white shorts, green trousers, and purple shirt.

I picked up his .45 from the top of the dresser where it had been lying. As he put on his brown shoes I checked the clip in the pistol. It was fully loaded. I might need all of the firepower I could get to get Leroy and me out of there. With my .38 comfortably resting in its shoulder holster and Leroy's fully loaded .45 in my right hand, I was ready to leave. I even had ice eyes' switchblade in my pocket if it came to hand-to-hand combat.

"Skip the tie and sports coat, Leroy. Move it." I waved the .45 toward the door.

I decided we would go down the stairs and out the front door instead of using the fire escape. I figured it for two of them in the front and one of them covering the fire escape in the back. Any way you counted it, it added up to three torpedoes that I would have to take. I would go where I thought most of them would be when I had the element of surprise. Besides, a guy coming down the fire escape makes a good target.

I was going to use Leroy as a shield, trying to keep him alive if possible. If he collected some lead, I could live with that. I had extracted some information out of him, but I would prefer to keep him around for further questioning and to identify the banker. If he took the big fall, it would give me relief from fighting the impulse to strangle him for what he had done to Irene.

Ice eyes was waiting for us in the front of the tenement. The driver was still in the car with the motor running. Leroy was in front of me and ice eyes couldn't see the .45 I held to Leroy's back.

"He wants to talk," I called to ice eyes who was less than fifteen feet away from me, standing by the Cadillac.

Ice eyes pulled out the revolver he was holding in his pocket and fired. He got off one shot before the bullet from the .45 hit him. I pumped a second .45 slug into him as he rolled against the Cadillac and fell. Ice eyes' aim had been as good as my own. Leroy staggered down the sidewalk, holding his belly.

The driver was harder to hit. He was on the opposite side of the Cadillac from me as he came out. I could run as fast as he could get out of the car. He was trying to pull his pistol out of his shoulder holster and turn toward me when I nailed him with the first .45 slug. I pumped a second shot into him as he lay on the pavement. That was something I had learned in the Marine Corps—always make sure your enemy is dead.

I heard a shot and looked up from my position at the rear of the Cadillac on the driver's side. Leroy fell this time. The torpedo who had just come around the building had nailed him again.

I couldn't get off a good shot from the rear of the Cadillac, so I crouched and started for the front. I don't know what the torpedo thought he was shooting at since I wasn't a visible target, but he fired two shots. As I stepped in front of the Cadillac, I straightened up and put a bullet in his heart. I knew that was where it hit because the Marine Corps had trained me to hit whatever I shot and I had continued to perfect that skill after the war. The torpedo dropped to the sidewalk without hesitation.

I hesitated a moment as my brain cleared to the situation. It had happened fast, but I knew the shots would soon be drawing people from the tenement. My brain told me to get out of there.

I bent over Leroy, lying face down on the sidewalk, and diagnosed him as dead. I placed the .45 in his outstretched hand and wrapped his fingers around it. I had his finger pull the trigger and fire the .45 in the direction of the torpedo I had hit in the ticker. The .45 jumped in his hand with my hand cupped over it and it flashed through my mind how ridiculous it was for me to be having one dead man shooting another. I knew what I was trying to do—make it look like they had killed each other—but it wasn't that clear in my mind. I left the .45 in his hand.

The Cadillac motor had purred through the whole thing. I stepped over its former driver and put myself behind the wheel. As I drove off in the lumbering, smooth giant, I saw where one of the bullets fired at me had hit; there was a hole in the right windshield.

The '48 Cadillac was comfortable and quiet, but it didn't seem as impressive as people had told me the '49 Coupe de Ville was. I had more important things on my mind, but I still wondered if the new Coupe de Ville hardtop was as great a ride as it was a looker.

Nineteen

It took me a long time to find my way back to my hotel. I had tried to keep track of our route when we had gone after Leroy, but I wasn't familiar enough with the city to keep things straight. Besides, my mind was not very much on driving as I tried to sort out what had just happened and what I should do next. I knew I was in deep trouble with the mob. Even if they and the police surmised that the thugs had done away with themselves, the mob would be wondering what had happened to me and what my part had been in the shootings. Maybe they would just forget it, but more than likely, they would want me dead.

The mob was smarter than I thought. When I arrived back at my hotel to pick up my suitcase and get out of New York as fast as I could, two guys were waiting for me in my room. I should have skipped the suitcase and the hotel checkout and just headed for Denver. Probably ice eyes was supposed to call his boss and tell him about the night's work. When he didn't call, they probably checked on ice eyes. They knew how to find my hotel faster than I did.

They made me face the wall and patted me down. The touch was so professional that I thought the guy who did it might have been a cop. I was sorry to part with my .38, which was put in the dark-gray suitcoat pocket of the guy who took it. I didn't mind them removing Leroy's switchblade. They motioned me out the door.

These two guys didn't talk and I couldn't draw them into conversation, which further fed my suspicions that they were cops. Cheap hoods usually like to shoot their mouths off about everything. Cops sometimes get in the habit of being quiet, maybe because when they are in the lower ranks, shooting off their mouths can get them in trouble with their superiors. These guys were dressed in dark-gray suits, which was typical plain-clothes cop attire. That was all I ever saw Harry Makris wear.

We arrived at the same liquor store where I had been before. The store was closed to business. This time, the room where the poker game had been was empty except for the guy who had done the talking the first time and two torpedoes who stood off to the side. The shades were drawn. The mob boss was still chewing on a cigar. It was unlit and I assumed it was not the same one he had had that afternoon.

"Mayfield, you're an inconvenience to me. You make me get out of my bed, leave my family, and come down here to see you."

"Why didn't you just have them bring me to your home? I wasn't going anyplace except where these guys took me."

"I never do business at home. Family and work are separate." His voice flashed in anger. "What went on tonight! Three of my boys are dead and you're alive!" I couldn't tell whether the change of voice was genuine or a planned tactic to intimidate me.

"We got there. Your boy instructed me to go up to the room, kill Leroy, and cut off his ear. I went up to the room. The girl who was with Leroy went running out. Leroy was tied to the bed in a most embarrassing way. I decided to let him get dressed before I killed him. I figure a guy should at least die with his clothes on. I cut him loose and I got careless. While Leroy was getting dressed, he slugged me. When I came to and went back to the car, Leroy and your three boys were dead. I got scared and drove off in the car. I was going to beat it out of town and back to Denver, but your boys stopped me and brought me here before I could leave."

He looked at the guy who had frisked me. "Does that agree with what you found?"

"It could. Leroy had a gun in his hand. The police lab will check out what the slugs in each guy were. From the position of the bodies, I would say Leroy could have been the shooter who got the other guys. They're crawling all over the scene now. I'll let you know tomorrow what they found out."

"What does Mayfield's gun show? Has it been fired?"

I almost smiled, thinking how lucky I had been, using Leroy's gun. I watched as my .38 was pulled out, passed around, and smelled. It was fully loaded and hadn't been fired in days. They all agreed that it was clean.

"If you're such a hotshot detective," the mob boss said, "how come Leroy was able to slug you? Why didn't you just kill him without his clothes on?"

I said it slow and with a touch of hurt pride to make it convincing. "I'm from Denver. As much as I hate to admit it, you guys from New York may be a little faster than I am. Look, I'm just a small time private eye from a hick town. I don't belong in New York City any more than one of our horses from home does. It just seemed the decent thing to do, let a guy die with his clothes on instead of tied naked to a bed. If I can get back to Denver, I'm going to kiss the ground and you're never going to see me in New York again."

"You know too much to let you go back to Denver." I figured he was going to have me killed, but I could see that I had him considering the possibility of letting me live.

"O.K., then knock me off. Let's get it over with," I demanded angrily, which was half real and half false. "Let's cut the bull. You've got my pistol. Let's see if you've got the guts to pull the trigger or have you got to have one of these bums do your dirty work?"

The eyes of the mob boss flashed in anger as he arched his black eyebrows. This time I knew the anger was genuine. "Who do you think you are, talking to me like that, punk? You're a small time private dick from a hick town and you think you can come to New York and talk to me like that!"

I cut him off before he could go on. "Ah, quit blowing. Let's get it over with. You know you're going to kill me. Either you pull the trigger here or have these guys bump me off someplace else. Dead is dead, and it doesn't matter a hell of a lot to me one way or the other."

"You really aren't afraid to die, are you?" I could see that I had him genuinely interested. I had myself interested, so I just spouted my philosophy of life.

"They nearly killed me in the war, but they didn't make it. When you come as close to death as I did, every day after that is a gift. I've had the gift, so I can be deep-sixed at any time and I'll have had more than my share."

"Where were you in the war?" the mob boss asked, genuinely interested.

"Iwo Jima among other places. You ever hear of it?"

"I heard," he said almost in reverence. "Did you raise the flag?"

"No. Only a few guys did that, but I saw it go up. I was there for twelve days until they carried me off the island."

"Can you prove that?'"

"Sure, I can prove it."

I didn't ask before reaching into my hip pocket and pulling out my wallet. I threw a picture of myself and two of my buddies in marine green on the table. It had been taken at Camp Pendleton before we had shipped out into the Pacific. They had both been killed.

"There, that's my family," I said angrily, deep emotions, long buried inside of me, welling up. "I don't believe in anything except the U.S. Marine Corps and the United States of America. You want to kill me; then do it. I been there before. There will be no family to miss me and damn few to mourn me. You think you hold the power of life and death over me. You don't because I died when those guys died and I'm just living on borrowed time."

It was quiet for a minute or so as I stood there, with them staring at me. I felt angry at myself for having opened so much of myself up to anybody, much less New York hoods.

The mob boss spoke. "Would you fight the Communists?"

"You're damn right I would," I said truthfully. "If those bastards try to take over the world, I'll beg the Marine Corps to take me back. If I'm not too old and they would have me, I would go in a minute. The Communists are just another group of thugs trying to take away our freedom."

The mob boss stood up. "I want to shake your hand," he said as he extended a hand. I could hardly believe it, but life has strange twists. Here I was in New York City, shaking the hand of a mob boss because we both disliked the Communists.

"I don't suppose you would be willing to go to work for me," he said as he withdrew his pudgy hand.

"No. You may be an American crook, but I still don't like crooks." He winced at the word "crook," but let it pass.

"Well, small time private detective, you've earned the right to live. You ought to take my advice and get married. A family can be a real comfort and joy. I know. If we were on better terms, I would introduce you to mine."

I said nothing, not knowing exactly how I felt or how to respond.

"You want a good time before you go back to Denver? Women? Booze? I like war heroes. I'll see that you get a couple of days of anything you want."

I thought a second. "No, but thanks. Maybe you're right about that family stuff. There's a lady back home I think is kind of special." I was thinking of Delana Dixon.

"Suit yourself." He handed my .38 back to the guy who had taken it from me. "Give it back to him when you dump him." He motioned his head for the guys who had brought me in to take me out. Maybe I was being a fool, but I really did think they were going to let me live.

"You know," I said, pushing my luck, "you should try the new Coupe de Ville. Your boys wheeled me around in a '48 Cadillac and I hear the '49 Coupe de Ville is really something."

"You like cars?" the mob boss asked.

"About as well as anything I know."

"You want a new Coupe de Ville?"

He saw me hesitate. "It will be clean and legal, papers and everything. I'll have my boys drop you one by tomorrow to drive back to Denver."

I knew I shouldn't take it, but I couldn't resist. "O.K."

"Take your Cadillac and go back to hicksville, war hero. If you ever show your nose around this town, I'll have your head blown off."

I nodded my head in agreement and left. They took me back to my hotel. I slept soundly, took delivery of the Cadillac the next day and started back to Denver. My trip to New York City had turned out in a way I never could have envisioned. The creme-colored Coupe de Ville with the deep blue hardtop and wide white sidewalls glided out of New York City as smoothly as if it had been riding on air. As it ate up the miles and I listened to dance music on the radio, I began to think of Iwo Jima. Blowing smoke rings from a Lucky and listening to the relaxing music, Iwo Jima seemed as far away as the moon.

Iwo had been hell on earth—sulfur rock with steam blowing in the air and the whole island honeycombed with Japanese, dug in like ants in underground tunnels and chambers. The Japanese thought it couldn't be taken in a thousand years, but we had taken it in less than a month.

Iwo was what the whole war was about, our flag or theirs. The Japanese had been putting their flag up and cheering, "Bonsai!" across Southeast Asia and the Pacific, not to mention Northern China. Well, we had taken their flag down and put up the Stars and Stripes. There would be no tears in the eyes of Americans as there had been in the eyes of the French when Nazi flags had been marched into Paris.

I thought of my buddies who would never see an American flag or any flag after Iwo. Tears formed in my eyes. I took a deep drag on the Lucky, trying to hold back the tears. Then I let them roll down because I was alone.

Twenty

When I arrived in Denver Joe Galliger and I took a late-morning ride in the Cadillac even before I went to my motel room to drop off my suitcase and clean up. I knew Joe would appreciate the Caddy.

"Sweet, Marty," he kept repeating as I poked at the gadgets on the dash and wheeled him out West Colfax toward the mountains. To hell with the rest of the world; it could wait while Joe and I played with the automobile. This was something new, a hardtop convertible, and a new Cadillac at that. New Cadillacs had been out of the reach of both of us.

"You want to drive it, Joe?" I knew there was nothing in life he would like better at the moment.

"You mean it, Marty? You'll let me drive it?"

I pulled the cream-colored beauty with the deep blue hardtop to the side of the road and got out, walking around the tailfins. Detroit had really come up with something this time. It was a two-door that looked like a sporty convertible, but really wasn't a convertible. Joe slid across the seat and planted himself behind the wheel. I could see the joy in his face as he pulled away from the side of the road.

"Jeez, Marty, what's in this engine?" Joe asked with satisfaction as we picked up speed. There was a look of complete pleasure on his face.

"It will do zero to sixty in about thirteen seconds. I tried it in Kansas. It'll do over a hundred miles per hour. I know, because I tried that in Kansas too. I eased up when it hit a hundred, so I don't know how much it will really do."

"Those cops in Kansas must love you," Joe said, lightening his foot on the gas pedal to slow down. My talk of a hundred miles per hour had scared him.

"That's how I got up to a hundred, outrunning one of them. He had a '48 Ford. He either couldn't touch me or he turned chicken. This baby has got 160 horsepower." I tapped the dash with satisfaction. "Drive it up to Central City. You've got time. Smitty can handle the lot until you get back. I can wait to clean up until we get back."

"I don't know," Joe said. "She usually only handles the paperwork. But I guess since Charlie comes in at noon she'll be O.K." He really did want to take a drive.

I leaned back with my scruffy beard, dirty clothes and all, but I was, as the farmer says, in hog heaven. I had slept three nights in the Coupe de Ville and it was like home to me. The seats were wide enough that a guy could really drift into dreamland. With burgers and coffee along the way, the trip had been a real pleasure, except for the gas bill. Money had never been a real concern of mine, so it didn't matter. If I had it, I spent it. If I didn't have it, I didn't spend it. "Who did you steal it from, Marty?" Joe's awe of the Coupe de Ville was leveling off enough for him to ask about the circumstances of its acquisition.

"It's legal and I've got papers and the title in the glove compartment to prove it. That's all I will say and that's all you want to know. I'll show you the title and the papers when we get back to the lot. In the meantime, let's enjoy the ride and the mountain scenery."

"Marty, you're one for the books. You make me nervous just living in the same state with you. O.K., but keep it at the motel or something. If somebody comes looking for it, I don't want it near my lot. I don't want them blowing up my car lot or roughing me up."

"I'll do nothing of the kind. I'll park it outside my office in open view. Relax, Joe; I tell you it's covered. Just make sure you don't get excited and sell it to one of your customers. I don't think anything would make me madder than that." I was needling Joe. I knew he wouldn't sell my car; then again, maybe he would.

"Jeez, Marty, what do you take me for? I never did a dishonest thing in my life."

"Yeah, Joe, I know, you and all car dealers."

We quit talking and concentrated on the ride and the beauty of the mountains. Almost August, the mountain grass was still green, but starting to dry a little in the foothills. It got greener the further up into the mountains we went. Pine and spruce dotted the mountainsides. Jagged rocks, huge boulders and mountain streams that collected on the canyon floor, remnants of mining operations—rust-layered equipment, abandoned and rotting ore-crushing mills with caved-in board walls and roofs, and cuts in the mountains, this was Colorado. What could be more perfect than a sunny ride in the mountains in a new Cadillac? A pretty dame instead of Joe Galliger's ugly face was the only improvement I could think of.

When we got back to Galliger's car lot, Joe confirmed that everything was as perfect as it seemed. The papers and title were legal; the Coupe de Ville was really mine.

Harry Makris was very interested in finding out where I had gotten the Cadillac. We were talking in a booth at the Red Horse over drinks, his bottle of Coors and my bourbon and water.

"Four torpedoes turn up dead in New York, one of them being a guy you went after. You turn up home with a new Cadillac and you won't tell me what happened or where you got the Cadillac; come on, Marty, you'll have to do better than that."

"Harry, believe me; you don't want to know. The Cadillac is legally mine. I had Galliger check out the title and papers on it. The world is cleaner because four thugs have been removed from it, one of them being Leroy. I'm home with a new Cadillac. Just be glad it turned out that way. Accept it the way the New York cops got it figured. The thugs knocked each other off, right?"

"Have you read the papers, Marty?"

"No, I haven't."

"When the story broke, that's the way the papers reported it. I checked with New York P.D., since we had an interest in Leroy and that's what they confirmed—it was a crime fight. They wiped each other out in an apparent gangland disagreement."

"If that's what the papers and the New York cops say, then, that's what must have happened."

"You took them, didn't you, Marty?"

"Harry, you're my friend, but you're also a cop. Stick with what the papers and the N.Y.P.D. told you. Leroy packed a .45. I carry a .38. They were killed with a .45. My gun is clean. It was never fired in New York. The mob certified my gun as being clean, probably the only gun around that has been smelled and certified by the mob. You want to smell it and certify it for the D.P.D.?"

Harry smiled. "I'll bet that's where you got the Cadillac too. You rub out four of their boys and they give you a Cadillac." He laughed. "'Marty, you're a one-man crime-fighting machine, and maybe a car thief who steals from the mob." I had never seen Harry so tickled.

"Harry, if what you say about the car has the remotest possibility of truth about it, I would appreciate it if you would keep it to yourself. Our local mob might get jealous and either try to rub me out or give me another Cadillac. I don't want the reputation or repudiation of associating with the mob. It's not good for business."

Harry laughed again and then turned serious. "Marty, I'll never spill it to anyone, not even my wife. Your safety is one of my primary concerns. Believe me, Marty, you don't make it easy."

"Thanks, Harry, I appreciate that. I could have used you in New York. I got a little nervous without being able to call you for back-up."

"Maybe we both would have got a Cadillac." Harry laughed uproariously at his remark. There was something about the mob and the Cadillac that struck him funnier than Abbott and Costello.

"How about another beer?" I asked to calm him down.

To my surprise, he drained the remainder of his bottle of Coors and said, "Why not?"

I motioned to Beverly, pointed at his empty beer bottle, and she brought him another. The new beer seemed to bring him under control.

"Did you find out anything about the banker?" he asked.

"A little, but not his identity. What I did find out is how Bobo and Leroy happened to be working for both the banker and the foreign agents. Leroy confirmed that they started out working for the banker. My guess is that the banker had contacted the mob for a hit on Irene and the professor, which they did for five grand a pop, with Leroy strangling Irene and then pulling the trigger on the professor. The banker hadn't decided whether or not he wanted Audrey killed, probably wanting to see what she knew about whatever it was Irene and her father were mixed up in. The banker had Leroy and Bobo shadowing Audrey while the banker made up his mind about whether or not to kill her.

"The foreign agents showed up on the scene and decided to kidnap Audrey. They offered Leroy and Bobo more money to go with them. They didn't really need Leroy and Bobo, but paying them better than the banker had paid them made it easy for Bobo and Leroy to get out of the way so the foreign agents could snatch Audrey. Since they had Bobo and Leroy on their payroll, they had them do a little guard duty at their headquarters. I happened to be at Audrey's when the foreign agents tried to snatch her, so they took me also. Since they had Bobo and Leroy hanging around, why not have them bump me off? Why waste good talent? I spoiled their plans by not getting bumped off, getting Audrey back, and causing their premature train deaths."

"But why did the foreign agents come into it at all?"

"Definitely uranium, Harry. I'll lay you a five spot that the professor had made a big discovery of uranium. What else would foreign agents be interested in, if not uranium for atomic bombs? We've got uranium in this state, and the Communists either want it for themselves or don't want us to use it."

Harry stroked his mustache. "No on your five spot, Marty. It makes sense. I don't donate five bucks to guys who drive Cadillacs. But, what's a banker doing in all of this?"

"My guess is that the banker is in on it for the value of the real estate. Wherever the professor found uranium, that ground is worth millions. As soon as the find becomes known, the value of that real estate skyrockets. The banker got the information of the find and tried to cut a deal with the professor and his daughter, if she knew about the find. Something soured the professor or he didn't go along with it in the first place, and he had Irene knocked off to keep the find secret. I haven't got all of the loose ends tied up yet, but my guess is that a banker is buying up a lot of real estate."

"Barry Hampton maybe."

"What did you and Delana find out while I was gone?"

"Some. but not enough to nail him or be sure he is the one we are looking for. Delana did get a job at the bank. She's been working in the real estate loan department where Irene worked. I tell you that woman is a smart cookie. She managed to get the job on her own and she's already into loans and has access to information on bank stocks."

"So, how close is she to getting the dirt on Hampton?"

"The Hampton family is in financial trouble, but they don't know it. Barry knows it, because he is the one who has tapped into family funds. He has a taste for high living and women. He's made bad stock deals and has no head for banking at all, only to authorize loans for his friends who have as little financial sense as he has. Barry has put the bank and family funds down at least three million bucks. When you're primarily a family-owned concern, that's real bad. The bank and the family fortune are almost broke."

"Well, Harry, I would say he sounds like our man."

"Being a bad businessman and ruining a family fortune doesn't necessarily add up to murder. Besides, he was in jail when the professor was knocked off."

"That's easy, Harry. He had already contracted with Leroy and Bobo for the job. Why the professor was at Sloan's Lake in the middle of the night, I'm not sure."

"We need more than what we've got on Hampton now before I can arrest him. Since somebody managed to kill both of the guys who could have identified the banker, we haven't got anybody to identify him. Nice work, Marty."

"Can you keep Delana digging in the bank longer?"

"It's already arranged. I talked to her boss Paul Horn when the bank hired her. He's willing to let her have up to a month to come up with the story. I think that's pretty reasonable of him."

"Are his lips tight so that he doesn't get her blown away?"

"They're tight. I impressed upon him the importance of silence. He doesn't want to endanger Delana any more than you or I do. I've been checking on her every day. I'm watching her as close as I can without giving her away."

"'That's good, Harry."

"I can tell you like this doll, Marty. I saw the way you looked at her and treated her when we were in the booth. Looks like a little romance, right?"

"Maybe. We're not ready to trip off into fields of flowers yet, but I'll call her now that I've checked out the situation with you. If I keep her away from where Barry Hampton might see us together, I suppose it might be safe to take her out."

"You and Barry Hampton don't travel in the same circles. Do you think he would ever be seen in a dive like the Red Horse?"

"Not likely, but I plan on taking Delana to someplace nicer than the Red Horse."

"Where's that, one of those Rocky Built Hamburger joints?" Harry laughed.

"No, Harry, I've got a little more class than that. I took her to Tyler's Supper Club before I left for New York."

"Not bad," Harry said with approval. "Charlene and I went there on our last anniversary. Maybe you and Delana can go there on yours."

"It's just a second date, if I can get her to go out with me again. Don't make more out of it than it is."

"Third date," Harry corrected, "here at the Red Horse when you invited me to discuss her banking job, Tyler's Supper Club, and now a third date."

"Harry, the Red Horse with her and you was not a date. You've been married too long."

Harry laughed and got up to go home to his wife and two kids.

A wife and two kids had always seemed like a trap to me. Seeing him leave, I thought it didn't seem half bad. That's what talking to a mob boss does for a guy. Maybe I should have never gone to New York and heard what the mob boss had to say about the comfort and joy of a family. When even a low-life crook could find good in it, there must be something to it.

Twenty-One

Delana was willing to go out with me. I set it up for a drive down to Colorado Springs. I wasn't a usual member of the crowd at the Builtmore, but I thought dinner and dancing there would be about as high-class as I could get. I had the Cadillac to go with the Builtmore crowd; I just didn't have the social connections.

I did have one connection at the Builtmore, Farley McDermot, who was an assistant manager at the resort hotel. Farley and I had driven taxis in Denver together while going to Denver University. I had quit D.U. to go into the detective business and Farley, having had a couple of years of college before the war, graduated with a degree in Business with an emphasis in Hotel-Restaurant Management. I knew because he had sent me a graduation announcement and I had watched him file across the stage and pick up his degree. It was knowing Farley that gave me the courage to go anywhere near the Builtmore. It was probably only knowing Farley that got me the reservation in the dining room.

Farley had insisted on reserving me a room when I had talked to him on the telephone. I didn't think I would be needing it, but perhaps the fires of romance would be lighted in Delana and we would use it. She seemed impressed when I asked her out and told her where I was taking her. She would have an evening of excellent food, champagne, and soft music in luxurious surroundings. I would even throw in some flowers.

While waiting the two days until our Builtmore date I busied myself with detective work and buying a tuxedo. The Builtmore was tuxedo territory and if you wanted to play, you had to pay. Farley, thinking I might not know this, had diplomatically advised me that I would need a tux and told me he would get me one to use if I didn't have one. I thanked him, but said I would come up with my own.

On the detective side of the ledger I indirectly pumped Frank Brodrick for information on the banker, but he offered none.

"I haven't got any idea who Bobo and Leroy might have worked for other than the foreign agents. What's it matter? You got them and the foreign agents who hired them to kill the girl and her father. Even if I did know anything about anybody else they might have worked for, I'm not sure I would let you have it. I stuck my neck out about as far as I could for you."

"Yeah, I know, Frank," I said, looking at the plate of eggs and flapjacks his waitress had just set in front of me. "As I've said before, Frank, I really appreciate it. Without you, I might have been nowhere on this case."

"They must have really liked you to give you that Caddie."

"Who?" I said, taking a forkful of flapjacks.

"Just certain people in New York."

I washed down the pancake mix with a swallow of coffee. "Patriotic, Frank, damn patriotic; it sure surprised the hell out of me."

"Guys on the wrong side of the law are still Americans. That's where Bobo and Leroy went wrong; they never should have worked for the Commies. That's how you were able to get to them so easy. Do you think the mob would have let you have them so easy if they hadn't worked for the foreigners?"

"Frank, are you sure you don't know anything else about Leroy and Bobo's working arrangements? I know we got them and the foreign agents, but I've got a gut feeling it just isn't wrapped up yet. Could there have been anybody else involved?"

"I told you what I know, Marty. It sure seems wrapped up to me. You got the Commies and the guys who killed the girl and her father. What more is there? Maybe it's like a good game of checkers. It's fun, but when it's over, you're sorry the game is over and want it to go on. You play checkers, Marty?"

"'Yeah, but not lately."

"I play every week. I belong to a checkers club."

"The hell you say."

"Maybe we can play sometime, Marty, when you're not busy on a case. I'll bet with that detective mind of yours, you're good at checkers."

"Sure, Frank, that's the least I owe you, a game of checkers."

I called Barry Hampton and asked him to meet me at a downtown restaurant. He had asked me to keep him informed, but that wasn't really the purpose of the meeting. I wanted to see how he was reacting these days and I wanted to see if I could draw anything out of him or find out something I didn't know already. I borrowed a '47 blue Chevrolet four-door from Galliger's car lot to drive. I didn't want Hampton to see or know anything about the Cadillac. I was waiting in a booth for Hampton when he came into George's Awful Coffee. That was the name of the place, but the coffee was really quite good, as was the food.

Hampton slid into the booth calmly and looked me squarely in the eye. "Well, Mayfield, what's up?" He placed his folded hands on the table in front of him. "Got anything else to tell me about the case? I thought it was over now that the other murderer was killed in New York."

"I suppose you read in the papers like I did what happened back there; I don't know anything more about it than that," I said, wanting to put him at ease and off guard. "I don't suppose I needed to ask you to see me about anything, but since we went through this whole thing together, I thought we might get together and talk about it or, at least, have a drink to celebrate the end of the thing. Can I buy you a drink?"

"It's a little early in the day for me, but I'll have a drink with you, Mayfield. You wouldn't be trying to butter me up to get some more money out of me for the other guy's demise, would you? Since, according to the papers it was some kind of a gang-land slaying that got him, rather than you, you can't expect to be paid for him."

"Really, Barry, would I do that?" I purposely used his first name to add a degree of familiarity.

The waiter interrupted us and we ordered drinks, scotch and soda for him and a bourbon and water for me.

"I just figured I owed you a drink. You paid me plenty for what I did. I'm not asking you for any money, but I'm not offering to give any of it back. It's nice to have my bills paid for a change. But I guess you don't have that kind of worry."

Hampton smiled. "You might be surprised. Life at the top isn't all that easy either."

The waiter set our drinks down and I continued with inane questions and buddy-talk that led nowhere. I couldn't get him to drink enough to get him drunk and I couldn't get him to reveal anything. I brought the conversation directly to the murders.

"Too bad about Irene and her father, but with the foreign agents gone and Leroy and Bobo gone, I guess that wraps it up. Anything about the case that seems puzzling to you?"

"Not in the slightest," he said with complete assurance.

"Well, for me, I still kind of wonder why they sat Irene's body up on the side of the road instead of throwing her over."

"I guess the criminal mind just can't be explained,"

Hampton replied with no show of emotion.

"Yeah, I guess you're right. That's something I'll never know."

Hampton stood. "Well, Mayfield, I've got to be running along. I work a couple of days a week in the bank. This is one of my days to work."

"Oh, really. I guess Audrey did mention that you are in the banking business. How's the banking business going?"

"Couldn't be better. As a matter of fact, things are really beginning to look up." He reached over and shook my hand. "Mayfield, it was nice talking to you. I guess this concludes our business. If I ever need a private detective again, you'll be first on my list. If you need me to recommend you to other clients, let me know."

I raised my glass to him and then drained the last swallow from it. I watched him go. He was still first on my list for the murders of Irene Berkowitz and her father.

I called before going to see Audrey. Any romantic enthusiasm I was kindling for her had been lessened by my interest in Delana, but I still wanted to see how she was reacting and to see if she had picked up any information that might be useful to me. She was still in the rented apartment in Golden and was at the kitchen table with books in front of her when I arrived. She looked like the schoolteacher that she was, but still attractive in jeans and a sweat shirt.

"Marty, how nice to see you. I've been going over some things for classes next year. It's not like home used to be, but if I keep busy, it makes me think less about Dad and Irene, and our family home that burned. With the insurance money they are going to be able to restore it. They are working on it now. The inside was gutted by flames, but the brick exterior held up pretty well. Of course, I'll never be able to replace the personal items lost in the fire."

"I'm sorry," I said, and I genuinely was.

"But life does go on, doesn't it. I'll be so glad when school starts. Teaching my classes hardly ever gives me time to think about myself. Would you like a cup of coffee?"

"Sure." I sat down at the kitchen table and waited for her to pour me a cup of coffee. She didn't ask if I took cream and sugar so I thought she must remember that I took it black on our train ride.

"How are things with Barry Hampton?" I asked

"Oh, fine, I guess. I see quite a lot of him."

"Any romance there?"

Audrey smiled. "Really, Marty, you are direct. I'm sure Barry sees a lot of other women, as well; that's just Barry. I learned that when he was married to Irene. As to whether there's any romance, we'll just have to wait and see."

She placed a cup of black coffee in front of me and, as if answering a sudden impulse, kissed me. I responded to the kiss and found her lips warm and moist.

She stepped back and looked at me. "That was just to say thanks again for my rescue from the kidnappers. About that time on the train, I just want you to know I'm not like that. I was frightened and had been through a lot when you rescued me. It just sort of happened."

"I know. Maybe I shouldn't have taken advantage of the circumstances, but I'm no saint and you are a very attractive woman."

Now I knew I was in trouble. My feelings for Audrey were heating up all over again. I was scheduled to take Delana to the Builtmore. Usually I didn't have any romantic interests and now I had, or at least thought I had, two women in my life who would make any guy ecstatic. Life can get complicated at times. I tried turning the conversation toward the original purpose of my visit.

"You saw where they got the other guy, didn't you?"

"Yes, I read about it in the papers." She sat down behind her coffee cup. "Was he the one who actually...oh, you know, my father and sister?"

"Yes, I think so."

"This sounds horrible, Marty, but I wish I could have been there to see him die. I know it sounds awful, but I would love to have seen him killed."

"I know, kid; sometimes somebody just makes you want to kick 'em in the mouth until they bleed to death. If it's any satisfaction, I can tell you that he didn't die a pretty death. Taking a couple of slugs is not overly pleasant."

"I'm glad."

"Sure, you're glad. Now it's all over. Feel mad and then heal. I hope you don't get hurt anymore."

"Why should I?"

"Just watch yourself with Barry." I didn't mean to say it, but I did. To cover the remark I added, "With a ladies' man and all, you've got to be careful. Don't let him break your heart."

"What if it's your heart I'm interested in?" She looked at me with those beautiful green eyes and I felt myself getting weak. I thought to myself maybe it was Audrey I should be taking to the Builtmore instead of Delana.

"Watch yourself on private detectives too, kid," I said as I stood up and swallowed the last half of the cup of black coffee.

"Are you leaving already, Marty?"

"I've got a busy schedule today. I'm working on some things. I wanted to see you, but I've got to get going."

I had to get going before I confused myself even more. I hadn't found out anything new on the case and had I found anything that was detrimental to Audrey, I couldn't have used it anyway. Audrey was too beautiful and nice for me to think any bad thoughts about her, even if she would have been an ax murderer, which I knew she wasn't.

"I'm looking forward to seeing you again, Martin," she said to me as if I were one of her students. She was a teacher who could keep me after school anytime and I wouldn't object. I gave her a wink and left before I got into anymore trouble with the teacher.

Twenty-Two

It was a warm August evening when Delana and I drove the seventy-six miles to Colorado Springs in the Coupe de Ville. The evening started perfectly. I picked her up at 5:30 P.M. and we were in the Springs by 7:00 P.M., the time which Farley McDermot had told me was the appropriate time we should arrive for the reservations I had made for the dining room. What Farley had failed to tell me was that there was a charity event scheduled for a banquet and ballroom next to the dining room.

The society swells were going into the Blue Room just as we were going into the dining room. Among those attending the Blue Room charity event were Barry Hampton and Audrey Berkowitz.

I saw them first and tried to move Delana into the dining room before either of them saw us, but the large crowd of society swells, milling in the lobby and swarming into the Blue Room, made a hurried entry into the dining room impossible. It was Audrey who saw us and pulled Barry Hampton in our direction. They overtook us just before we entered the dining room.

"Marty," Audrey called and I had little choice but to stop and turn around. The look of surprise on Audrey's face was as great as the surprise registered on Hampton's face and my face.

"Marty, what are you doing here?"

"Yes, Mayfield, what are you doing here?" The tone of Hampton's voice was that of catching me somewhere I didn't belong.

"Delana, may I present Miss Audrey Berkowitz," I said, trying to remember the proper form of introduction they had tried to teach us in the seventh grade. "Miss Audrey Berkowitz, this is Delana Dixon. Her gentleman escort for the evening is Mr. Barry Hampton."

Delana extended her blue-gloved hand toward Audrey's green-gloved hand and the two of them shook hands formally. "How nice to meet you, Miss Berkowitz," Delana said. "I know both of you indirectly. Miss Berkowitz is, I am sure, the same Miss Berkowitz of Mr. Mayfield's recent case. I've seen Mr. Hampton in the bank where I am employed. I doubt that he knows me, but all of the bank employees know Mr. Hampton."

"Oh, but I have noticed you, Miss Dixon." He took the blue-gloved hand and briefly touched it to his lips. I couldn't remember having learned that in the seventh grade, but I had seen it done in the movies, so I assumed it was what someone born to the silver spoon would do.

The four of us stood there awkwardly for a few seconds, two stunningly beautiful women, dressed elegantly in evening gowns and wearing orchid corsages, and two men dressed in black tuxedos. Delana's evening gown was midnight-blue and she had matching midnight-blue earrings and gloves. Audrey's evening gown was emerald-green and she wore gold earrings and emerald-green gloves that matched her evening gown.

"Are you here for the charity ball?" Hampton asked. I knew he knew that I wasn't, so why did he ask? I decided he was trying to needle me.

"No, just dinner and dancing."

"We have dinner and dancing also," Audrey said. "Perhaps they could join us, Barry."

I didn't think she was needling me. The way she looked at Delana I could tell she was curious about my date. I could understand the curiosity. Why would a guy like me be at a place like the Builtmore with a gorgeous woman like Delana? Had I been there with Audrey, the questions would have been the same.

Since Hampton delayed in making a reply, Audrey continued, "Please, Barry. I really don't know any of these people and it would be nice to have some ordinary people like myself around. I don't mean that unkindly, Miss Dixon, but if you are a working woman like I am, we really are an oddity here. Barry's friends are always so wealthy."

Delana smiled. "The remark is taken as it is intended. I would be happy to join you and your escort in dining and dancing if my escort, Mr. Mayfield, and your escort, Mr. Hampton, are agreeable."

With the two women making a pact, what could Hampton or I do? I tried one last stall. "I have reservations in the dining room and they are not expecting us at your charity ball; won't that throw the seating arrangements off?"

"Nonsense," Audrey said. "Barry can attend to it. With a few words to the management and the people who arranged the ball, Barry can have that changed. Barry is very influential. I'm certain management would be more than willing to cater to his wishes."

I thought of Farley McDermot and I knew she was right. Farley knew how to treat the swells swell; that's one of the things they had taught him in Hotel-Restaurant Management.

"It shall be as you request, my dear," Hampton said, starting to steer us through the crowd in the direction of the Blue Room. I didn't like the sound of that. I hoped he wasn't setting me up for an embarrassing evening. I hoped I could pick up on their lead enough to know which fork to use.

As we went into the Blue Room I thought of how incongruous the situation was. I was eating dinner with the guy I was trying to nail for murder. Previously, I had broken his nose in a fight. Later, he had become my client. He was escorting a woman who was the sister and daughter of the murder victims. I had made love to her and I was not totally innocent of harboring thoughts of making love to Delana this night. Delana was pretending to be a bank clerk, which she was, but not really. She was a reporter who was trying for the big story. She knew and I knew that Hampton's finances were not as hot as he pretended. He didn't know that we knew, so he could sit on his pretended-throne of wealth and peer down on us peasants; which I probably was, since I could hardly remember the proper form of introduction. Delana, on the other hand, coupled with the peasant of the evening, had during her time in Washington, D.C., been at gatherings where Hampton would have been the peasant. Audrey was just an innocent schoolteacher caught between peasantry and royalty. It seemed like a very strange evening, indeed.

The women seemed to get along wonderfully, I was the only one who did not have much to say. I couldn't match Hampton in his cocktail repartee, so I didn't try. I was on his playground, so all I could do was parry when he made a verbal thrust at me. In a back-alley fight I could take him anytime. Here, I could only try to hold my own.

Farley McDermot made no personal reference to me when he made the change in seating arrangements. "Mr. Hampton, I've informed the Dining Room Captain and I'll have the gentleman and his lady seated at your table." Farley hid his surprise well.

"Excuse me," I said, "but didn't you attend D.U.? You

look familiar to me. I may have seen you on campus when I attended there."

"That's quite possible, sir," Farley said with a tone of professionalism. "I was graduated from Denver University with a degree in Business Administration with an emphasis in Hotel-Restaurant Management."

"A fine school and a fine degree," I said.

"Now, if you will excuse me, sir, I have my duties to attend."

As Farley walked away, Hampton said, "What were you doing at D.U.?"

"Studying."

The dinner went reasonably well. I merely watched Delana and did as she did. I used a similar small fork or big fork whenever she did. As we went through the courses of the meal, I was sure she was a good guide, having received a degree from Stanford and having been married to an Army captain on General Marshall's staff. In an etiquette battle with Barry Hampton, I would put my money on her.

The biggest surprise for me came at the end of the dinner when the swells made their pledges to the construction of a home for the aged. Five hundred dollars and up was the going rate, with most being in the thousands. Hampton pledged two thousand. My name had been added to the guest list, so it was called at the very end by the chairman of the charity event. "Mr. Martin Mayfield."

"Five hundred dollars," I called back.

Audrey looked across the table at me. "I'm sorry, Marty. I didn't know." The look on Hampton's face told me he enjoyed the gouging I took in the interest of charity. I was sure he knew about it from the moment he had my name added to the guest list. Delana seemed surprised that my name had been called and that I thought I could come up with the minimum donation.

"That's O.K., Audrey; I'm sure you didn't."

"Part of the fees I paid you, Mayfield?" Hampton asked.

"A fool and his money are soon parted," I replied. Hampton didn't know whether I was referring to him or me. Actually, I think I was referring to both of us. I would make good on the pledge, even though I was spending the money I had earned from Hampton faster than I had earned it. My check would be in the mail to the Colorado Springs Bank the chairman of the charity event had designated as the collection point for the funds.

The dancing part of the evening went more smoothly because I didn't have to converse much with Hampton. We exchanged dances and I found Audrey as stimulating to dance with as Delana.

Audrey wanted to know where I had met Delana and I responded I had once known her from a case. It was a lie, but I wanted to keep Delana's cover at the bank.

"Do you get to know all of your former clients on a social basis?"

"No, just the beautiful ones. That's why I came to see you the other day." That wasn't totally true either, but what was a guy to do in a situation with two women he found equally attractive?

Late in the evening I used Hampton as an excuse to get Delana to stay the night. "If Hampton stays the night, do you think it might be useful to hang around to see if we can learn anything more about him?"

Delana looked up at me from her dancing position. She gave me an amused smile. "Marty, that's the lamest excuse I ever heard for trying to get a woman in bed."

I started to mumble an apology and she took her hand from mine and placed a finger on my lips. "Darling, I've been married and I've been around a little. I don't plan to get married again, but with the right guy, I could have a long-lasting relationship. That includes sex. Shall we see if we are compatible?"

"Yeah, sure," I said, guessing she meant that she would spend the night.

I felt her gloved hand caress the back of my neck. I had not mistaken her meaning.

"And just how do you plan to get a room?" she whispered in my ear.

"That guy I know from D.U., I'll talk to him and see what I can do."

"Don't let him hold you up too much. If you have to tip him an outrageous sum, a motel will do fine. If you are a little short on money with all the expenses, let me know; that's the advantage of dating a working woman."

I excused myself and went to Farley McDermot in his office in back of the main desk in the lobby. I let him know I would be needing the room.

"You're one hell of a mover, Marty. How did you get in with that crowd? The woman you are escorting is absolutely beautiful. That one your friend has is a knockout too."

"See what happens when a guy quits college, Farley. You stayed and all you've got is this hotel."

"It has its compensations. I've used the same room you're going to use." He handed me a key to room 505. "That's first class, my friend, and not everybody gets it at the regular room rate you're getting it at."

"Thanks, Farley. If you ever want a drink at the Red Horse, I'll buy."

He laughed. "You still hanging out at that dive?"

"Nothing but the best. I seem to remember another cab driver who used to drink there with me."

"Those were good times, Marty, tough times, but good times."

I nodded my head in agreement. After a few more sentences of conversation I went back to the ballroom.

When the dancing was winding down, Audrey suggested we all go to the coffee shop before starting back to Denver. Hampton didn't look very pleased with the suggestion, but Delana put his mind at ease.

"Audrey, that is a wonderful idea, but I really need to be getting back. If you'll excuse Marty and me, we'll be leaving now. Audrey, you and Barry have been most gracious to us and we have had a lovely evening. That is right, isn't it, Marty?"

"Yes, a very nice evening." I was left with little choice other than to thank Barry Hampton for his hospitality, even though I knew it had been forced.

We exited the ballroom, but instead of having my car brought around, we went up to room 505. It was all that it should have been, with a view of the lights of downtown Colorado Springs. Delana was impressed enough to ask, "Just how much did you have to tip that guy?"

"Whatever it was, you're worth it."

As Delana removed her earrings, she said, "The advantage of having a woman like me is that I can be discrete. And by the way, I thought your manners were impeccable."

"I learned them in the seventh grade."

She smiled. "I saw you looking at my forks and spoons. "Was it that obvious?"

"Not at all; just to me because I wanted to jump in and help you if you needed help."

"Did you mind that I might have needed a little coaching?"

"Not in the slightest."

"We just might be compatible," I said, taking her in my arms.

I kissed her and then I watched her put a black high heel on the vanity stool and roll down her nylon stocking.

I took pleasure in knowing that as I was enjoying Delana and one of the finest rooms in the Builtmore, Hampton would be driving back to Denver. The five hundred dollars I had pledged to the old-age home was well worth it. I had never known that helping old people could be so rewarding.

Twenty-Three

Three days later Delana made the find we had been looking for. Barry Hampton had been buying all the land he could get in the area surrounding the dinosaur tracks. He had been buying the land in the name of the Westview Development Company. Land titles were registered in Jefferson County to Westview Development Company, with banker Barry Hampton acting on behalf of the Westview Development Company. Loans to purchase the properties were made from bank funds at an extremely low interest rate.

On the surface, most of this was legal. There may have been a question of improper use of bank funds, or perhaps even fraud, but those were matters for state or federal bank regulators. All of this did not add up to a murder conviction.

Harry Makris did not have any evidence that would make it worthwhile to arrest Hampton.

Harry, Delana and I huddled at the Red Horse to figure out our next move. I sat on the side of the booth with Delana, looking across at Harry. I enjoyed the closeness of Delana but knew that Harry had the more pleasant view. That was O.K.; he could look, but not touch.

"We still don't know that he is a murderer," Harry said. "I'll admit we have good reason to suspect he has inside information on all of the land he is buying, but that doesn't make him a murderer."

"Delana and I went up to the dinosaur tracks this morning with a Geiger counter and what do you think it showed?"

"Uranium?"

"It was hotter than a pistol. As you probably know, Harry, a Geiger counter measures radiation or something like that, which is indicative of uranium. Delana and I used the thing up and down the Hogback and it wouldn't stop clicking. We went as far as two miles east of the Hogback and found the same thing. Maybe Hampton is buying all of that land about fifteen miles out of the city for future home development, say in about forty years or so. Then again, maybe he's interested in farming or cattle raising; which to me, not knowing much about either, doesn't look overly promising in the area."

"Don't ask me," Harry said. "I'm a city kid. Delana?"

"Barry is not the type for either farming or ranching, so it really doesn't matter."

I continued with my analysis of the purchase of the land. "I doubt that anybody else knows about the uranium in the area or they would be bidding up the land. Delana says he has spent less than fifty thousand dollars so far to buy the land and the few houses in the area. He can't go very far west because that is where Red Rocks Park is and that is owned by the city of Denver. What puzzles me is why he even needs loans. Fifty thousand bucks seems like pin money to Hampton."

"Not so," Delana corrected. "The family fortune is far worse than I originally thought. Barry has all but depleted it."

"Then why did he pledge two grand to the old-age home when we were in the Blue Room?"

"Appearances, my darling. Didn't you notice that two thousand dollars was a little low by some standards? The top people brought their pledges in at about ten thousand. Barry, to keep his standing in high society, had to come up with at least two thousand dollars. I'll bet I can find a loan at the bank for it."

"So, now it's darling." Harry looked amused. "You two must have gotten along pretty well at the Springs."

"Harry, you're a nosy cop, too nosy. O.K., Delana, if his funds are so low, why did he pay me so much?"

"Maybe his funds weren't that low then. Maybe it was worth it to throw you off the track."

"As you recall, Marty, he was sitting in jail, being grilled by you and me when he offered you the five grand to take him as a client. He was in a tight spot. A guy in jail, suspected of murder, is willing to pay for his release. I wonder if he can still afford the attorneys he had then."

"Got any ideas as to what we can do to nail him, Harry? I've got one that involves Delana, but I don't like it."

"I can put a tail on him. Delana can keep digging at the bank until her time runs out and she has to go back to the paper. That's about all I know to do. I don't think we want to make public what we suspect about the land around the dinosaur tracks."

"What is your plan that involves me?" Delana looked at me with trusting eyes, which made me feel guilty about the plan my brain had devised. My heart and my brain were not working together.

"Delana, I'm not sure I should even suggest it. It's about the only thing I could think of that might get Hampton to reveal his guilt. Actually, it is not only risky to you, but it may even be stupid."

Harry chuckled. "Well, it seems you've outdone yourself again."

"O.K., wise cop, you come up with a better one."

"Let's hear yours and I'll see what I can do."

"Hampton has a reputation as a ladies' man. That's what got him in trouble with Irene. By the way, that's how he married someone who was not of his social standing. Irene worked at the bank, and being a beautiful woman, Hampton dated her and even went so far as to marry her. Then he started playing around on her and got their marriage in trouble."

Delana interjected, "You can't totally trust any of them. The male of the species is a wandering animal."

I ignored the comment and went on. "I saw the way Hampton looked at Delana when we were in the Springs. He's very interested."

"I didn't want to tell you how interested. I thought you might want to punch him or something, but since you weren't the one who had to dance with him, I thought I would leave you out of it. Besides, I thought you showed some interest in Audrey."

"Nothing offensive," I said.

"Who said, offensive? I just said Barry was interested in me."

"Interested enough to ask you out?"

"More than enough."

"If you were to set him up for Harry, then maybe we could get him to reveal whether or not he was behind the murders. Here comes the part I don't like."

Harry leaned forward. "If you don't like it, it must be good."

"I'm intrigued," Delana said.

"You probably won't be by the time I get through explaining it to you. Joe Galliger has a cabin up Turkey Creek Canyon. He uses it sometimes on the weekends, usually just Sunday, mostly in the summer. It's a place where he can go and relax. Joe loans us the cabin. Delana takes Hampton there. Harry has staked the place out with a couple of his boys back in the trees. Harry is inside the closet..."

Harry groaned. "Delana tells Hampton what she thinks she knows, and I jump out and arrest him. I don't like it. You're right; it is dumb. It sounds like something an amateur would dream up. You must have seen too many Saturday-morning movies when you were a kid. Even if it did work, juries are beginning to frown on that sort of thing. Leading a suspect into a trap like that may someday be illegal."

"Yeah, just like your guys can't roust a guy and use a little physical force to get him to confess—you think that might be illegal too. Come one, Harry, if we can get Hampton to admit guilt and have witnesses, Delana, yourself, and maybe even Joe Galliger, no jury in the state would fail to convict him."

Harry looked at Delana. "Now he's got Joe Galliger in the closet with me." He looked at me. "I like it less all the time, and just what makes you think Hampton will spill the beans to Delana?"

"When she tells him what she knows and then asks to be cut in on the real estate profits, he'll talk. If we are anywhere near right, and I think we are dead on the money, he's either got to talk about a deal or deny that he is involved in anything. A denial brings the risk of Delana going to the police. He doesn't know that we suspect him of being behind the murders. Why would he want Delana making such charges to the police and getting the police involved?"

"What if he decides to kill her?"

"That's the part that bothers me."

"It could be a concern of mine too," Delana said with more of a touch of humor than alarm.

"That's why you're there, Harry. I said I would trust you with my life. I trust you with Delana's life. You've got your back-up out in the trees someplace and I'll be coming along."

"'Where are you in all this while I'm in the closet?"

"I assume Hampton has never seen my Cadillac. If I thought he had, I would just borrow a car from Galliger anyway. I think a Cadillac is the last car he would suspect to see me in, so my Coupe de Ville is a good choice. I'll tail them from the time he picks Delana up. Why? I want to cover the risk of him deciding to take her someplace else. If he changes plans, I don't want Delana to get worried that somebody won't be keeping an eye on her. I doubt that he will suspect anything, but if he does, I don't want any harm to come to Delana."

"How nice," Delana said. I couldn't tell whether the remark was sarcastic or teasing.

There was silence while Harry played with his mustache. I said nothing, thinking that I had probably already said too much. Maybe I had blown my relationship with Delana. I wanted to pin a murder rap on Hampton, but I could see where a plan like this could really make her mad. Suggesting she go out with a murderer was not the way to foster our relationship. Furthermore, I didn't like putting her at risk of the wrath of Barry Hampton. I should have kept my mouth shut and let Harry work on it in his own way.

"I'll do it."

Harry and I were both jarred out of our thoughts.

"I can entice Barry to the cabin. I can get him to talk. I will be surrounded by protection. You will get your murderer and I will get and be part of a very big story. The newspaper will love me. It's a great plan, darling; I couldn't have done better myself."

"She may be right, Marty. Dumb idea, but I think it will work. I think we can keep her safe and get our man, if he is our man."

"But what if he pulls a gun and tries to blast her?" I asked, giving in to my concern for her safety and trying to raise objection to the plan I had just proposed, but wished I hadn't.

"He's not going to carry a gun on a date. Would you or I carry a gun if we were going to where Delana is taking him with what he has in mind? Did you take your rod with you to Colorado Springs?"

"It was in the glove compartment of the Coupe de Ville. You're a nosy cop."

"That's my business. If I'm not being nosy, I'm not doing my job."

"But what if he suspects something before he picks her up? Then he might be packing a piece, and then you run the risk to Delana and yourself."

"She yells. I come out of the closet. I've got the element of surprise. It's not the way he operates. He hired people to kill Irene and her father, if he's our man. Carrying a weapon is not only bad manners on a secluded date; it just doesn't fit the man's society profile or the way he has done things in the past."

"Maybe Delana won't even be able to get him to take her to the cabin," I said, still looking for a way out.

"Now I am hurt. Wouldn't you take me to a secluded mountain cabin?"

"Maybe we ought to just cancel this whole idea and you and I will go there and Harry can go home to his wife."

"O.K., love birds, let's get to work on the details." Harry was enthusiastic, but not about the same thing I was. "Let's see if we want to modify your plan. Let's coordinate our efforts and decide when and how is the best time. Delana needs to know how she can signal us if it's off. She needs to get straight the story that she is going to tell Hampton."

I interrupted him. "Just typical police stuff." The remark didn't even slow Harry down.

Twenty-Four

At 10:07 on a sun-laden Sunday morning the '49 cream-with-blue Coupe de Ville and I began to tail the '48 black Chrysler business coupe with Hampton and Delana in it. I tagged onto them a couple of blocks from her home, with the tail running loose because I had the presumed destination. That way I didn't have to run the risk of following too closely and tipping him off. If I lost the Chrysler for a little while, I just picked it up further along the route. I could tell it had an automatic transmission by the steady, not-too-fast acceleration it had when it took off from stop signs and stoplights.

The Chrysler business coupe convinced me that Hampton really was a banker. I had expected something with a little more flair. Black, with all-black tires, the Chrysler looked fairly plain. I kind of liked the long hood and heavy chrome grill and bumpers, but I was a sucker for most cars, even the ones that still carried a design that was mostly pre-war. Chrysler had done a little better with its '49 models.

The fact that Hampton was driving a '48 instead of a '49 also told me his financial fortunes had been sinking. No self-respecting, family-fortune man would be driving a car that was a year old rather than a new car.

The good thing about Hampton's banker-black car was that I knew the Caddie could outrun it with no problem if tail came to chase.

We left Denver and headed into the mountains with the Coupe de Ville still hanging back. As we neared the turnoff to Turkey Creek Canyon I tightened the distance between us. I wanted to be able to see him make the turn into Turkey Creek Canyon. If he missed the turn, I wanted to know.

The Chrysler did not turn into Turkey Creek Canyon and I began to sweat, even with the windows rolled down. Delana could be in danger. I hoped Hampton had just been a poor navigator rather than someone with malice in mind.

I had to stay fairly close, following at maybe six or seven car lengths. I didn't want to miss any sudden turnoff he might make on the occasional dirt roads that ran through the green pine and spruce trees and down the mountainsides to the road we were on. If I stayed close enough and lost him around a curve, I would still probably be able to catch the turnoff by the dust that would be kicked up from where he turned.

Hampton speeded up. He knew I was following him. The plan had backfired. Neither he nor Delana looked back, which told me he could be holding a pistol on her with one hand while driving with the other. Otherwise, why would she not be glancing back to perhaps signal me in some way?

We were doing close to sixty on a road where the speed limit was forty. I could have had the Coupe de Ville overtake the Chrysler at any time, but I held back, fearing he might panic and perhaps shoot Delana or have an accident with the car. Steering with one hand, even a car with an automatic transmission, was not the safest of practices.

The Chrysler cut off onto a mountain road, showering dirt and dust into the air. The Caddie made the turn and I was eating dust all the way up the mountainside, bouncing on a rutted, rocky road that was not made to be climbed at thirty-five miles per hour. Any faster than that and it would have shaken the best of cars to pieces, which included the Coupe de Ville.

We reached the summit and started to wind down the other side of the mountain, the road being no better on that side than on the other side. I could see a small ranch house in a clearing below before the descent blocked the view with tall stands of pines.

By the time we reached the ranch-house clearing, the Coupe de Ville was less than three car lengths behind the Chrysler. I had pulled closer, thinking that if an opportunity to make a move came, I would make it.

At that distance I could see Delana's face clearly. Her gaze was fixed on Hampton and she did not look back at me, further confirming that he was holding a pistol on her.

As we passed the ranch house it looked deserted and in disrepair. We went past a falling-down corral and then splashed across a stream that had bedrock for the road, but probably had a wooden bridge over the bedrock at one time. Cutting into the trees again we followed a winding road that caused us to slow down to no more than twenty miles an hour. My guess was that it had been a logging road, probably used to drag logs to the ranch. We wound up and over a hill. The narrow road curved right as it started in a steady descent down the hill. A washout of rain and mudslide or snowslide had cut the road in two. The Chrysler could go on if it could fly over the chasm of maybe twenty feet to the other side. Hampton wisely stopped the car.

Delana seized her opportunity and fled from the passenger side of the car. Hampton, hemmed in by the drop off on his side of the road, slid across the front seat toward the door where Delana had just exited.

As Delana started toward me I pushed the accelerator of the Coupe de Ville to the floor, cutting the wheel to the left enough to miss her. I was halfway out the door when the Coupe de Ville smashed into the Chrysler, taking the Chrysler, Hampton, and itself into the chasm. I felt myself falling free of the Coupe de Ville, and then hitting my head on dirt and rock. That was all I remembered until four days later.

When I awoke in the hospital I learned from Delana that Hampton was dead, crushed by the falling cars. Before I drifted back into unconsciousness or sleep, or a combination of both, I decided it was a waste of good cars, but necessary. In my delirium I kept running after the Coupe de Ville, trying to stop it from falling into the chasm.

Twenty-Five

It was late September when I was released from the hospital. Colorado had a chill in the night air. Colorado could turn cold or snow at a September-moment's notice or it could hold the bad weather until Christmas. Sometimes, the snow hit abruptly. At other times, a freeze didn't come until October or later, and Indian-summer days could make you think winter was never coming. The only predictable thing about Colorado weather was that it was unpredictable.

The four of us gathered at the Red Horse to have a postmortem of the case. The gathering of Delana, Harry, Audrey and myself was at my request. I thought it was important that Audrey have all the information concerning her father's and sister's death so that she could put them to rest. I had learned in the war that when somebody you care about dies, knowing what happened makes it easier for you to give them an honored place in your memory and get on with your own life.

Another reason for the gatherings was my own interest in putting everything together. The concussion I had received had made me less-than-clear on everything myself. Now that I was coming back together in both mind and body, I wanted to exorcise the spirits of what in my mind I had started calling while lying in bed and trying to get my brain to function "The Dinosaur Tracks and Murder Case."

As we sat in the booth, I was on the side with Harry. I was on the outside, thus permitting my straight left leg in a cast to be propped up on the chair that Red had supplied. My head was still bandaged. Why? I wasn't sure. The only other injury was my broken left little finger that had a splint that made it stick out straight. I was in a blue sports shirt and black slacks that had the left leg cut out for my leg cast. Delana had seen to it that I had clean and cut clothes to permit me to go out in society. I had stayed at her apartment the three days since my release from the hospital.

Harry was wearing one of his dark gray suits, as always. Audrey, sitting across from Harry, was dressed in what I assumed were teaching clothes—maroon skirt and blouse, plaid yellow-and-black vest. Delana was wearing newspaper clothes, a blue suit; I knew they were newspaper clothes because she had just barely had time to come from work and get me to our six o'clock Red Horse rendezvous. I was the only one dressed for leisure, but what could you expect for a Tuesday night?

Audrey sat facing Harry, and Delana faced me. Since I had asked for the gathering, I began the discussion of the case.

"Audrey, I wanted to get together to help you have everything clear in your mind about what happened. Maybe you know all of it; maybe you don't. I've been kind of out of it, so I'm not really sure what any of us knows, including myself."

Audrey smiled. "Marty, you really are a nice guy. I think I've got it all pretty well sorted out, but it's helpful to talk about it. Delana's newspaper story was very complete. But you know, Delana, I still don't know where Dad's uranium find was."

"You didn't tell your readers that?" I asked.

"I thought I would discuss it with you first, to decide whether or not we make it public. There are three of us who know—you, Harry and I. I think Audrey has a right to know; do you agree?"

"Absolutely," I said. "Harry?"

"Absolutely; it was her dad's find."

"Audrey," I said, "your dad's uranium find was up around the Hogback, where they found Irene's body."

I looked at Audrey before going on to see if the mention of Irene's body upset her. She seemed to have gotten to the point where it could be discussed without her showing noticeable outward emotion, although I knew it must still hurt her inside.

"Your dad found uranium. He told Irene. Irene told Barry Hampton. Hampton wanted to make it pay off. He tried to convince your father and Irene to keep it quiet while he bought up the land in the area. Your dad balked, for whatever reason I'm not sure, maybe just scruples."

I took a small swallow of the bourbon and water sitting in front of me and then looked at Harry. "You tell me if you think I've got this figured right. Hampton decided to kill Irene and the professor when they wouldn't go along with keeping the find quiet until he could make millions out of it. Hampton was on the Hogback the night Irene was killed, not because she had asked to meet him there, but because he had asked to meet her at Lovers' Point to talk about a reconciliation of their marriage. Bobo and Leroy were waiting at Lovers' Point to kill Irene, having been hired by Hampton to do so."

Harry nodded his head in agreement.

I looked at Audrey. "This may be a little tough to hear, but it is what I think happened. After Leroy strangled Irene, Bobo, thinking your sister was very beautiful, would not let Leroy throw the body over the side. Instead, Bobo found a place by the side of the road and propped the body up in a sitting position, allowing, in his mind, Irene to look out over the lights of Denver. It is my guess that he also thought the body would be seen there and given a decent burial. That's why I could be somewhat charitable in my opinion of Bobo when I told the newspapers about him. Mixed up as he was in your sister's death, he didn't do the actual killing and tried, in a bizarre way, to make some amends for what had been done."

Audrey nodded and then turned her head toward the wall of the booth. She took the paper napkin that Beverly had placed under her coffee cup when she had brought it and daubed at her eyes. The front of my head was starting to ache, so I welcomed the pause from thought. When Audrey seemed sufficiently composed, I continued.

"Barry Hampton went to the Hogback to see if Bobo and Leroy had left any telltale signs where they had committed the murder. To his consternation, he saw Irene's body sitting on the side of the road under the dinosaur tracks. He did slip and fall when trying to pick it up, and bumped his nose, causing it to bleed. That is how he got blood on Irene. He tried to pick her up, not to put her in the car as he claimed, but to throw the body over the side where it wouldn't be found. Seeing his blood on Irene panicked him and he left. He was arrested by the police. Harry, could you go on with the story? I'm feeling a little tired." It wasn't a feeling of tiredness that made me stop as much as the throbbing pain in the front of my head.

"Sure, Marty; you O.K.?" Delana and Audrey were looking at me anxiously.

"Marty, do you need to go home or to the hospital?" Delana asked.

"No, just tired of hearing myself talking; that's all." It was true, but it was also a lie.

Harry set his Coors bottle down and then spoke. "Hampton had already contracted for the death of the professor. The professor was probably told to be at Sloan's Lake at midnight if he didn't want anything to happen to his other daughter. He went and Leroy shot him."

"In a sense, I killed Dad," Audrey said.

Delana quickly said, "No, Audrey, you can't look at it that way. They would have killed your father at some other place or found another way to lure him wherever they wanted him. They killed your father. He went to Sloan's Lake because he loved you. He didn't want any harm to come to you. He must have been a very good father."

Audrey stared into her coffee cup. "The best."

Harry went on quickly. "Then it was Marty to the rescue. Hampton hired Marty to guard you after Leroy and Bobo had been hired away by the foreign agents. They had been shadowing you while Hampton waited to see how much you knew about your father's uranium find. Hampton eventually decided you didn't know anything, so he wouldn't have to kill you. The foreign agents weren't sure you didn't know anything, so they grabbed you with the intent of taking you to East Germany and finding out what you did know. Marty stopped that. Hampton had only hired Marty to draw suspicion away from himself as a murder suspect, but Marty was up to the task of taking out the foreigners."

I nodded at Harry. The pain in my head was easing some now that he was doing the talking.

"Marty not only took out the foreign agents, but he got rid of the thugs as well."

"Both of them?" Delana asked.

"Don't print it," I said. "The newspapers got it right. I got Bobo. The mob got Leroy."

"That's right," Harry said. "That's what I meant—Marty got Bobo and the mob got Leroy."

"Then, why did someone give Marty a Cadillac?"

"Delana," I said, my head starting to throb again, "drop it. The way Harry told it is the way it is."

"I'm sorry, Marty," Delana apologized.

I wasn't sure what she was apologizing for, but I smiled at her to let her know it was O.K.

"That is when you let me in on the case. I dug in the bank and found out about Barry's financial problems and his buying land in the area of the dinosaur tracks. Marty devised a plan and it didn't quite work like we planned, but we got him."

"Why didn't he turn off at Turkey Creek Canyon?" I asked.

"Barry Hampton was a ladies' man and he was very perceptive about a woman's feelings. I thought I had him roped into a rendezvous with just my charm. He discerned that my feelings weren't genuine. When we left Denver he said, 'I know you have an ulterior motive in wanting this date with me. What is it you really want?' After denying several times that I wanted anything other than his affection, he threatened to turn around and bring me back to Denver."

"So, you went ahead and gave him the story we had worked out," Harry said.

"I thought I could still get him to go to the cabin and maybe we could still get him."

"Instead, he didn't turn up Turkey Creek Canyon and Marty pursued him to the end while I waited in the closet with Joe Galliger. I never have told Joe what we were doing in that closet, and I don't think I will."

"At least you and Joe didn't end up in the hospital like I did. I can't clearly remember what happened. I remember following Hampton all the way up onto a rough mountain road. I remember Delana getting out of the car and coming toward me. Then I go blank. Delana says I rammed the Coupe de Ville into the Chrysler."

Harry reached his hand across his chest and patted my shoulder in an uncharacteristic way. "You sure did, old buddy. You don't need to remember. You got that son-of-a-bitch and saved the state a lot of money. I'm sorry, ladies; I meant son-of-a-gun."

Audrey nodded her head and said, "You said what he was. I won't repeat it, but that's what he was. Thank you, Marty, for all you've done."

"It wasn't much, and I am glad to have done it. I will miss the Cadillac, but I guess I'm not really in the Cadillac class, so it doesn't really matter." I was kidding myself. I knew I would mourn the Coupe de Ville for many months, if not years. "Something else puzzles me; how did I get to the hospital?"

"You weren't the only one who was heroic." Harry reached across the table and laid his hand briefly on Delana's wrist. I had never seen Harry as demonstrative as he was tonight. He was the kind of cop who really did appreciate any help people gave him in laying the bad guys to rest and tonight he was showing it. "I've got to hand it to you, Delana; you know how to think in a crisis."

"What crisis?" I asked.

"The one you created by nearly killing yourself by ramming your Caddie into Hampton's car so far away from where you could get medical attention. Marty, you're a lucky man that Delana is not the type to sit and cry. It might have taken days to find you on that logging road. Delana managed to get to you—I estimate you had fallen and rolled a hundred and ten feet from the point of impact. Delana propped your head up so you wouldn't strangle in your own blood. After checking your injuries, she did what she could to keep you warm by removing her white sweater and covering as much of your upper body with it as she could in the hope that you wouldn't go into shock and die while she was gone."

"Where did she go?" I asked.

"Six and three-quarters miles out to the main road, that's where she went. She walked it barefoot, carrying her black high heels. She was wearing her black skirt, nylon hose and her white bra. How many other women would have given you the sweater right off their back to keep you warm? How many women would walk barefoot six and three-quarters miles to get you medical attention? Her feet were bloody from the walk by the time she reached the road."

Delana interrupted. "Really, Harry, you are making it sound more heroic that it was. We women are not just ginger and spice and everything nice. We can act when we have to."

"That's telling him," Audrey said. Audrey's approving smile told me that the two of them had become sisters in arms. Pity the poor man who got in the way of either of them. I hoped they retained the ginger and spice because I had always thought women were everything nice. I wouldn't live in a world without them.

"Just the same," Harry continued, "I think it was damn heroic. Standing by the side of the road in just a bra and skirt, Delana didn't have any trouble stopping the first male motorist who came along. As he took her toward Denver she saw one of our squad cars by the side of the road. We were searching the area without much success in trying to determine what had happened to you and Hampton. We didn't even know for sure that Hampton and you had made it into the mountains. Without Delana walking back to the main road and leading us to you with medical help, you probably would have died there."

I reached across the table and placed my hand on top of Delana's hand. She turned her hand over and I continued to hold it. "I guess I owe you more than I realized."

"No debts, Marty. You don't owe me a thing. I got my story. We had a few laughs, a little danger and a little romance along the way. What more could a good reporter asks for?"

"Just my gratitude, and you have it."

"Too bad it cost you your Cadillac, Marty," Harry said.

"Is it totaled?" I asked.

"Let's just say you or no one else will ever drive it again. What about the insurance? I couldn't find a record of any."

"I don't think I had any, as nearly as I can remember. I didn't have the car that long and I just hadn't gotten around to getting it yet."

"That's why someday there will be a law that says everybody who owns a car has to have car insurance. They laugh at me at the station when I tell them this, but it should be a law to at least have the other guy's car covered by your insurance."

"Oh great, now I can pay Hampton's heirs for the loss of his Chrysler."

"I didn't mean that, but you get the idea. I'll be happy to enforce such a law if they ever pass it."

Delana said to me, "I'm sorry about your Cadillac, Marty. It was a beautiful car."

"Ah, what's a car? It doesn't keep a guy warm when he's between the sheets." Normally, I wouldn't have said something like that, but my head injury had caused me to be less guarded in my comments. I think it was a combination of not being aware of social conventions and using the head injury as an excuse to get away with anything I wanted to say. It was kind of like being a lecherous old guy of ninety and finally getting to say the off-color things you had been thinking for years, without anybody getting mad at you now for saying them.

"I'll do that," Delana said.

"What?" I asked.

"Keep you warm between the sheets."

"Maybe I want to do that for Marty," Audrey said.

The two women looked at each other and smiled. Harry tried to look like he wasn't there, which he couldn't. I just looked pleasantly surprised.

"You can share me," I suggested, trying to get away with my ninety-year-old-man routine.

"Maybe we will," Delana said.

"Maybe we will," Audrey agreed.

Had I been ninety years old, I probably would have had a heart attack. As it was, I just smiled and thought of the good times that I hoped awaited me. If I lived to be ninety, I might have plenty to remember.

I don't suppose we lived happily ever after, but 1949 was a good year. We agreed among ourselves to not tell about the uranium up around the dinosaur tracks. Why should we let anybody spoil perfectly good dinosaur tracks for uranium? The Cold War, uranium, and a beautiful woman found dead under dinosaur tracks on the Hogback—that was 1949, and we solved the case.

I suppose the uranium is still there because time doesn't

move things like that, only people do. The dinosaur tracks will eventually fade if not preserved—rain beating upon the rock, snow falling, melting, and freezing, sun baking the rock— hundreds of years, thousands of years, millions of years, who knows? It is enough for now that the murderers paid for their crimes and the dinosaur tracks remain.